ROCKY MOUNTAIN MADNESS

BROTHERHOOD PROTECTORS COLORADO BOOK #6

ELLE JAMES

TWISTED PAGE INC

ROCKY MOUNTAIN MADNESS

BROTHERHOOD PROTECTORS COLORADO
BOOK #6

New York Times & *USA Today*
Bestselling Author

ELLE JAMES

Dedicated to my father and mother for introducing me to adventure at a very young age. Camping vacations were so much fun for us and gave us a great appreciation for nature and getting to know different places. I miss you both every day.
Elle James

AUTHOR'S NOTE

Enjoy other military books by Elle James

Brotherhood Protectors Colorado
SEAL Salvation (#1)
Rocky Mountain Rescue (#2)
Ranger Redemption (#3)
Tactical Takeover (#4)
Colorado Conspiracy (#5)
Rocky Mountain Madness (#6)
Free Fall (#7)
Colorado Cold Case (#8)

Visit ellejames.com for titles and release dates
For hot cowboys, visit her alter ego Myla Jackson at
mylajackson.com
and join Elle James's Newsletter at
https://ellejames.com/contact/

PROLOGUE

"LAST NIGHT, my wife told me we're expecting kid number two," Dustin "Dusty" Benton said as he slid onto the bench seat in the Black Hawk helicopter next to Cole. "She has a whole list of honey-dos for me when I get home."

Bryce "Cole" Coleman's hand clenched around his M4A1 rifle. Three years seemed like a long time. It wasn't long enough. No matter how many days went by between his thoughts of the past and what he had lost, it only took one comment from a teammate to send him back to that day three years ago when he'd come out of a fierce battle in Helmand Province only to be met by his commander and the chaplain with devastating news.

Dusty must have seen the strain in his face. "Sorry, man. Sometimes, I forget."

Cole shook his head. "Don't be sorry. I'm happy

for you, Kim and Katie." He really was happy for them. Dusty had a wife, a kid and another on the way. Who wouldn't be happy?

Had Lisa and baby Tyler lived through the tragic fifty-car pileup on Interstate 25 that icy day in Colorado Springs, he and Lisa would've had a couple more kids by now.

Lisa had been seven months pregnant with their second child and had been on her way back from a play date at a friend's house in Monument just north of the Springs. She'd left early when a freak ice storm swept in from the northeast. Hoping to get back to Fort Carson before the roads got bad, she hadn't known the snow falling north of town was ice further south. With temperatures below freezing, the ice had stuck to the roads.

When the drivers had encountered the ice, they hadn't been able to slow down to avoid hitting the vehicles in front of them. They'd skidded sideways and rammed into each other. Lisa and Tyler hadn't had a chance. The eighteen-wheeler behind them slammed into her small SUV. Their only saving grace was that they must have died instantly.

Even though he'd been rushed back to the States, the funeral had been closed-casket as their injuries had been so catastrophic, the mortuary hadn't been able to piece them together for a family viewing.

He hadn't been able to see them one last time or say goodbye. It hadn't felt real. It had been as if they'd disappeared and left an empty hole in his heart.

"What are you hoping for?" Cole asked out of politeness and to prove to his battle buddy that he had moved past his grief—which he hadn't.

"Kim wants a boy," Dusty said. "I thought I did too...you know, to carry on the family name. But after having Katie, I could totally love another baby girl." He grinned. "You know my enlistment is up at the end of next year. I'm thinking of getting out of the Army."

Cole snorted. "And do what? We're soldiers; all we're trained to do is fight."

Dusty glanced over at Cole. "You remember Max Thornton?"

With a frown, Cole nodded. "I remember Thorn. He trained us in mountain climbing. Fell from a two-hundred-foot cliff and broke damn near every bone in his body."

"That's him," Dusty said.

"What about him?"

"He was medically retired. He recovered, for the most part, and went to work for an organization called Brotherhood Protectors."

"Glad he recovered and found work," Cole said. "He was a good guy."

"Yeah, one of the best. What's cool is that he's using his military training to protect, rescue and help others."

3

"So?"

"So, I'm going to see if they have room for someone like me. That way, I'm not deployed three hundred and sixty-five days a year. I might get to watch my kids grow up and be there for their birthdays, ballgames and dance recitals."

"Sounds too good to be true," Cole said.

"I checked it all out. Even called his boss, Jake Cogburn. He's a former Navy SEAL. He said I should call him when I get closer to mustering out. I'm going to do it." He turned toward Cole. "What about you? Aren't you due to reenlist in a couple of months? Ever thought about getting out and actually having a life?"

His job in the military had given him the refuge he'd needed to get away from the pain. When deployed, he didn't have to see the highway where Lisa and Tyler had died. He didn't have to drive past the house they'd lived in on post. Deployment meant no reminders of the family he'd lost. "This is my life," he said.

"I haven't said anything to Kim because it's still a year out, but I'm going to do it." Dusty grinned and settled back as the helicopter engine revved and the rotors spun.

It was like Dusty to talk about anything but the mission ahead. It helped to keep the nerves from getting to him. By the time they neared the drop zone, he was all about the task ahead.

Cole focused solely on the task, which was how he preferred it. He didn't have anything else to think about. After Lisa and Tyler had died, he'd moved into a one-room apartment he rarely saw and volunteered for every deployment. Anything to get him away from Colorado Springs and the family he'd lost.

This time, they were headed into Somalia on a mission to extract a medical doctor who had been taken hostage from a Doctors Without Borders aid station the night before. Between intelligence personnel on the ground and satellite images, they'd located the village where the doctor had been taken by members of the terrorist organization, al-Shabaab.

Their mission was to sneak in, grab the doctor and get out as quickly as possible.

Because the ten-man team from the 10th Special Forces Group had been the closest geographically, they'd been tasked for the mission.

Satellite images of the village indicated no more than a dozen militants. Intelligence on the ground had spoken with displaced villagers who'd said the leader of the al-Shabaab group was one on the list of their most wanted.

Though their primary job was to retrieve the doctor, taking out the terrorist leader would be a bonus.

The Black Hawk slowed and lowered to the ground in a field a mile from their target and on the other side of a hill. The clear night sky gave them the starlight they needed to find their way through a field and up the hill, where they stopped to study their target.

All was quiet below until movement caught Cole's attention. He lowered his night vision goggles and spotted the heat signature of a man leaning against the side of a building, holding an AK-47 rifle.

Cole spoke softly into his microphone. "Bogey on the north entrance."

"Another on the south exit," Dusty's voice sounded in Cole's headset. "And a man standing guard in front of a small structure."

Cole motioned to Malcolm. "Alpha team, take the north." He turned to Rocha. "Bravo, take the south entrance."

The biggest hut in the village had been identified as the one the al-Shabaab leader occupied. They'd locked the doctor in the small hut beside the larger one. It had to be the one with a guard standing in front of the door.

While the other team members took out the sentries on the road, Cole and Dusty moved into the village, working their way past several huts to the one with the guard.

Coming in from behind the structure, Cole took the right side, Dusty the left.

When they were even with the front, Dusty tossed a pebble in front of the guard.

The man who'd been leaning against the door straightened, bringing his weapon up in his arms.

Cole moved in from behind, his knife drawn. Before he reached the man, an explosion rocked the ground beneath him, and the night sky lit up.

The guard spun toward the sound, caught sight of Cole and whipped his rifle toward him.

Dusty was on him before he had the chance to pull the trigger. With his Ka-Bar knife, he dispatched the terrorist and leaped past him to the door.

Cole was there first. He kicked the door open, knowing they only had seconds to get the doctor out before all hell broke loose.

He rushed into the tiny hut with its dirt floor.

A man in a dirty white lab coat and blue scrubs struggled to his feet and toppled over, his wrists and ankles bound with zip-ties.

Cole bent and, with his knife, sliced through the plastic, freeing the doctor's feet. The man held out his hands, and Cole cut through the binding.

Gunfire rattled to the north.

Cole darted for the exit.

"We've got company," Dusty said from the doorway and opened fire into a group of men streaming out of the larger hut. "Get ready to run!"

With his left hand, Dusty yanked a grenade from his vest and pulled the pin.

"Get down," Cole shouted. He dropped to a

crouch and covered his ears. The doctor followed his lead.

With his right hand, Dusty fired into the group of men as he ran to the side of the little hut. Then he tossed the grenade and ducked behind the wall.

The explosion shook the hut, and dust rose in a cloud around them.

"Go!" Dusty shouted. "I'll cover."

Cole grabbed the doctor's arm and ran through the door and around the opposite side of the little hut.

The doctor moved slower than Cole would have liked, limping as he ran.

When Cole looked back, Dusty followed, stopping to lay down fire and keep the enemy at bay.

Cole and the doctor made it to the edge of the village as the chopper hovered in a clearing at the designated extraction point fifty yards out, lowering to the ground.

"My team's coming in hot," Malcolm said over the radio. "Did we get the package?"

"Got the doc," Cole said. "Headed for the pickup."

"Bravo's free," Rocha said. "We're close. We'll cover."

"Watch for Dusty," Cole warned. "He was right behind me, taking fire."

"Roger," Rocha responded.

Cole glanced at the doctor. "Can you make it?"

The doctor nodded.

"Let's do this."

As they started to run, the doctor tripped and fell to his knees.

Cole looped his rifle over his shoulder and bent to help the man to his feet. Then he draped the doctor's arm around the back of his neck, wrapped an arm around his waist and ran with him.

Though gunfire sounded behind him, Cole kept moving. When they reached the helicopter, he shoved the doctor into it and turned.

Alpha team knelt or lay in the dirt, their weapons trained on the village and the Somali terrorists shooting toward them and the helicopter. They were far enough away that the bullets didn't reach the aircraft.

"Dusty, report," Cole said into his mic.

When he didn't respond, Cole's gut clenched. He ran toward the village. "Anyone see Dusty?"

"Saw him a minute ago," Rocha responded. "He was between us and the guys behind that hut shooting at us."

"Coming in from the north," Malcolm reported. "Got one injured."

Cole made it to Bravo Team's line, dropped to the ground and pulled down his night vision goggles. As Rocha had indicated, several enemy combatants were using a hut on the edge of the village for cover, darting out periodically to fire at them. Between the hut and Bravo Team lay a heap on the ground, generating a green heat signature.

"Shit, shit, shit," Cole muttered. "Cover me."

He leaped to his feet. Crouching low, he fired continuously at the building as he raced for the man lying in the dirt.

Bullets hit the ground around him, launching puffs of dust in the air.

Cole couldn't think about them. He had to get to his friend, his battle buddy, his brother.

When he reached him, he dropped to the ground beside his friend. "Dusty, buddy, you gotta get up."

Dusty lay on his belly, his cheek in the dirt. "Did you get...the doc?" he asked, his voice weak, barely a whisper.

"He's on the chopper. That's where you need to be, dude. Get up."

"Too tired," he said.

Cole rolled him onto his back. The ground beneath him was stained black with his blood, most of which had been absorbed into the dry earth.

Bullets flew over Cole's head. He didn't give a damn. This was Dusty. He couldn't leave without him. "Come on, man. It's time to get out of here."

"Need sleep," his friend murmured. "Baby's crying."

"Kim and Katie are waiting for you. You have to move."

"Tell Kim..." His voice faded.

"You can tell her yourself," Cole said. "You're going home to her and Katie."

"I love...her..."

Cole had to lean close to hear Dusty's last word that came out on his last breath.

"No." He shook Dusty gently. "Goddamn it, you cannot quit on me now. Damn it, Dusty, you have to make it home. You have a baby coming. Kim needs you to help change diapers. Katie loves her daddy." He fought back the tears and failed.

Dusty lay still.

Cole felt for a pulse at the base of his neck, knowing he wouldn't find one but praying he was wrong.

Through it all, bullets flew over his head and pinged the ground around him.

Rage burned in Cole's chest. Why Dusty? Why did Dusty have to die? Why couldn't it have been him instead? Why hadn't he been there for Lisa and Tyler?

The anger flamed through him like a wildfire. He grabbed his rifle, lurched to his feet and ran toward the hut the al-Shabaab fighters hid behind. He fired again and again until he'd emptied his magazine.

Still running, he ejected the empty magazine and slammed a full one in its place. And he kept firing.

A man hiding behind the building leaned out with his rifle.

Cole roared his anger and cut him down. Another

man emerged and fell. The third man barely made it around the corner before Cole took him out as well.

He didn't realize the gunfire had stopped until he rounded the far corner of the hut. The last of the enemy fighters were running away.

Cole roared again, shooting at their retreating figures.

"Cole, it's time to go," Malcolm said over the radio. "We have a man needing medical attention...Cole!"

He lowered his rifle and turned around. "Coming," he said. He walked back to where Dusty lay, not caring if the enemy returned and shot him in the back. At that moment, he wished they would. Then he wouldn't have to live to tell Kim her husband was dead. He wouldn't have to see the confusion on Katie's face when he told her that her daddy wasn't coming home.

The bullet in his back didn't come. He was alive when he should have been the one lying on the ground.

"You got Dusty?" Rocha asked, shaking Cole out of his trance.

He couldn't die now. He had one last task to accomplish. "Yeah," he said into his mic.

He had to get Dusty home.

CHAPTER 1

THREE MONTHS LATER...

"Can I get another whiskey?" Cole banged his empty glass on the bar. One drink hadn't been enough to take the edge off the day. Two wasn't much better. At three, he was just beginning to feel numb.

"Sorry, soldier," the bartender said. "I'm cutting you off." He took the empty glass from his hand. "Now, you can either order something to eat, or I can call a taxi to get you home."

"I don't need a taxi," Cole said, the anger that had been his constant companion since Dusty died flared. "I don't need a ride, and I don't have a home. I just want a goddamn drink!"

The bartender crossed his arms over his chest. "Not going to happen. You need to go home and sleep it off." He picked up the phone. "I'm calling a cab."

"Don't need a cab. I have my own wheels."

The bartender frowned. "Really? Show me your keys."

Cole slid off the barstool and nearly fell. He straightened and pulled the keys out of his pocket.

The bartender reached across the bar and snatched the keys from his hand. "You aren't driving anywhere. I'm calling a taxi. I don't give a rat's ass if you kill yourself, but I won't let you out on the road to kill someone else."

"Give me my keys," Cole said.

"You're not driving, and if you don't calm down, I'll call the police, and you can have a nice warm bed for the night in jail."

"Keep the keys," Cole said. "All I wanted was a drink." And to forget. He spun and walked toward the door. Maybe if he walked far enough, he would end up on Interstate 25, and a truck might hit him and put him out of his misery.

As he stepped through the door, he tripped over his own feet and would have fallen but for the two men who caught him and stood him straight.

"You okay?" the dark-haired man asked.

"Yeah. I'm fine. Just effing fine." He started to

14

move past them when the other guy grabbed his arm. "Coleman?"

Cole looked into the man's face and blinked. If the whiskey hadn't been messing with his vision, he could swear the guy looked familiar. "Do I know you?"

The man nodded. "You were on my mountain training course a couple of years back." He held out his hand. "Max Thornton."

Cole's frown deepened as he tried to wrap his foggy brain around the name. It wasn't quite right. The man's name was shorter... "Thorn?"

He grinned. "That's what they call me."

Cole gripped his hand. "Thought you broke a few bones."

Thorn nodded. "I did. But I'm doing better. Can we buy you a cup of coffee?"

Cole glanced toward the other guy. "I'd rather have whiskey."

"If not coffee, how about a hamburger?"

"You buying?" He snorted. "'Cause I'm tapped out. Only have enough cash for one more drink."

"I'm buying." The dark-haired man held out his hand. "I'm Jake Cogburn."

When Cole didn't grasp his hand, Jake leaned closer, took his hand and shook it. "It's a pleasure to meet you, Mr. Coleman. Where can we get a decent hamburger around here?"

Cole couldn't remember why, but the name Jake

Cogburn sounded familiar. "Not here. The staff steals your keys." He nodded toward another building. "They serve burgers across the street and breakfast twenty-four hours a day."

"Sounds good," Thorn said. He gripped Cole's arm and started to cross the street.

Cole pulled free. "I don't need your help." He stepped off the curb in front of oncoming traffic he hadn't seen a moment before.

Jake and Thorn grabbed his arms and hauled him back up onto the sidewalk.

Once the cars drove by, Jake and Thorn walked with Cole to the other side of the street and into the café. That's when Cole realized both men walked with distinct limps. It was kind of ironic that they were helping him cross the street and not the other way around. Funny, they didn't seem to need his help, and twice since he'd run into them, he'd needed theirs. That didn't sit right with Cole. He'd never needed anyone's help.

For the first half an hour, neither man said much other than to order food and drinks.

Cole ordered a hamburger, fries and black coffee.

Jake ordered eggs over easy with bacon and toast.

Thorn asked for a cheeseburger.

While they waited for their food, Cole studied the two men, wondering why they'd asked him to share a meal with them.

He was just about to ask when the waitress arrived and set their plates in front of them.

Cole hadn't realized how hungry he was until then. He didn't care why the men were there as long as he got to eat the hamburger and fries first.

Ten minutes later, Cole sat back, full, and just a little bit soberer than he'd started. "So," he said, "what are you selling? I'm not buying because, like I said, I'm about tapped out."

Jake pushed his plate aside and leaned his elbows on the table. "You recently left active duty, right?"

Cole nodded. "Yeah, so?"

"Found work?" Jake asked.

His eyes narrowed. "Not yet."

"I heard your last mission was a tough one," Thorn said.

Cole shrugged. "It's classified. I can't talk about it." He didn't want to, even if he could.

Jake stared into his eyes. "You lost a friend in that mission, didn't you?"

His frown deepened.

"You went to Dustin Benson's memorial service today?"

Cole's chest tightened, and his eyes burned. One more word from them, and he was out of there.

"I bet as you stood there, you felt like you should've been the one buried," Jake said quietly.

Cole pushed back from the table so fast his chair fell backward. "Yes, I wished I could take his place.

His wife and children needed him. He died, and I lived. Why? I have no one who needs me. No family was waiting for my return. Yet, I came home on my own two feet, and Dusty came home in a body bag. It should've been me." He spun and started for the door.

"I've felt the same way," Jake called after him. "I lost friends in battle. Friends who were my brothers. When I lost my leg, I wished I'd lost my life instead. I crawled into a whiskey bottle and wallowed in it for months. I couldn't get work. I was a Navy SEAL with combat skills I could no longer use and missing a leg."

Cole's heart beat hard against his ribs, and he halted. The anger that had erupted was quick to subside, leaving him spent and...sad.

"The point is, I had nowhere to go. No one wanted to hire me, and I had no purpose in life. I was ready to end it until a man named Hank Patterson sent someone to find me.

"Hank was a Navy SEAL as well until he went home to Montana. He found a way to use the skills he'd learned as a SEAL to help others who can't help themselves or need help to help themselves. Please, Cole, hear us out."

Tired of fighting. Tired of hating himself for living when his friend died. Tired of feeling lost, he turned back, righted his chair and sat. "I'm listening."

"Hank started a security agency called Brotherhood Protectors. He hires former special forces soldiers, SEALs and Marines who have the tactical and strategic combat training to help people."

"Help people?" Cole asked. "How?"

"Some need personal protection, like a body-guard. Others need to be rescued from dangerous situations here in the states or wherever we're needed. Not only are we providing a service to people who need it, we're employing veterans for the skills they acquired from combat." Jake's lips twisted. "I can see by your expression that you're skeptical. I was, too. Until my first assignment." He smiled. "It became clear that there was a need, and even a one-legged former SEAL could satisfy that need."

"We'd like you to join the Brotherhood Protec-tors," Jake said. "We need men like you with your skillset."

"Patterson started this business?" Cole asked.

Jake nodded.

Cole crossed his arms over his chest. He had no intention of taking the job, but he was curious. "Why didn't he come to do his own recruiting?"

Jake nodded. "He's in Montana, running the orig-inal branch of the Brotherhood Protectors there. They're growing so fast he sought me out to head the Colorado division. I didn't want the job."

"But you obviously took it," Cole said.

"On a trial basis," Jake admitted. "I didn't think I could add value. I proved myself wrong, and now I manage this branch. I can make my own hiring decisions, and I'd like to hire you."

"Thanks, but no thanks." This time when he stood, the chair didn't topple over. "I'm not a charity case."

Thorn snorted. "We wouldn't be offering you a job if we thought you were a charity case. We know your reputation and skills. You're exactly what we need."

Cole shook his head. "Not interested."

Jake held out a business card. "Keep my card and think about it. You can call me or show up at that address if you decide to accept our offer."

Cole started to hand the card back to Jake.

"I'm sorry about your friend, Dustin Benson," Jake said. "I'd hoped to bring him on board when he completed his enlistment. He would've been an asset to our team."

Cole's throat tightened to the point he couldn't breathe.

In that instant, he was back in that helicopter sitting with Dusty as he'd talked about his plans for the future and how he was going to work with Brotherhood Protectors.

He'd never had the chance to realize that dream. Now, Cole was in a position to follow through on his friend's vision of the future, and he was going to walk away?

Oh, hell no.

Cole tightened his jaw. "I don't need to call you. I'll join. But not for me. For Dusty. It was his dream. The least I can do is live it for him."

"Glad to hear it." Jake stood and held out his hand. "Welcome to Brotherhood Protectors. You can start tomorrow morning. Sober."

CHAPTER 2

"DR. MILLER, you're needed out at the Glory Hole Mine." Elizabeth Severson poked her head into Dr. Staci Miller's office. "One of the miners was in an accident."

Staci closed her computer and grabbed the satchel her father had gifted her with upon her graduation from medical school. That bag had become her mobile doctor's office, containing as many supplies and medications as she could carry to cover the most common ailments and injuries encountered in the small Colorado mountain communities she'd visited over the past six months.

The small office the community members had given her was nothing more than space carved out of a storage closet in the only lodging facility operating in Glory Valley, Colorado. She'd been there two weeks, and the work had been constant as if the people had saved up all their medical issues for the moment a doctor just happened to come to town.

The nearest medical clinic was a two-hour drive through some of the curviest switchback roads Staci had ever traversed. She could understand the people of the community postponing a visit or "toughing it out" rather than making the all-day trip down and back up into the mountains.

In Glory Valley, she'd discovered babies were delivered by midwives. Her temporary assistant, Elizabeth Severson, was one of the four midwives who served the community's medical needs with home remedies and over-the-counter medications. She was efficient and effective at working with people, but she didn't document anything.

Oh, she had patient history, but it was all stored in her head.

In her medical training and residency, Staci had it drilled into her to document every patient interaction. This documentation could reveal a trend or unveil a deeper-lying problem when all the pieces of the puzzle were examined and put together.

Staci could access none of that knowledge without asking Elizabeth. At the end of each patient visit, Staci made it a point to chart the visit and any tidbit of information Elizabeth offered.

In the thirty-five patients she'd seen in the last two weeks, some had come to her office. In many cases, she'd gone to the patient's home because he or she was too ill to come into town. Elizabeth accompanied her on all visits, as she was most familiar with all the people in the valley, knew where they lived and the best way to get there.

Staci was thankful she had a four-wheel-drive SUV. Some roads weren't roads at all, but rutted paths leading up to ramshackle homes kludged together with logs, plywood and sheets of tin. She'd even been in a few that still had dirt floors.

Glory Valley was somewhat hidden high in the Colorado Rockies at elevations ranging between nine and ten thousand feet above sea level. Only one way in through a mountain pass often meant the people living there were cut off during the long winter months. The people lived off the land as much as possible, growing their own food and canning and drying meats for use during the winter.

According to the community leader, Cyrus Severson, there were two hundred and eighty-one people living in the valley. At the height of the gold rush era, the valley had been home to nearly ten thousand people working the mines or supporting those people who worked the mines.

The community had one schoolhouse teaching all levels. The houses in town had electricity and running water, but many outlying families burned wood for heat, had outhouses and still hauled water from wells.

Staci had never experienced this level of poverty

in her own county, having grown up in a high-end gated community. She'd attended the best private college-preparatory schools and had lived a gilded life.

After her graduation from high school, Staci had gone on a backpacking trip in the mountains and had run across a town tucked into the hills much like Glory Valley, where children had run around barefooted and dirty, and they'd lived in homes with dirt floors. Some had skin conditions that made their lives miserable; others had broken bones that had mended untreated, making their arms or legs misshapen.

Appalled at what she'd witnessed, Staci had vowed to do something to help. In college, she'd studied pre-med biology. On summer breaks, she'd worked with Habitat for Humanity, building homes for the homeless.

In medical school, when she hadn't been buried in her studies and clinicals, she'd volunteered at a free clinic doing health screenings.

Upon receiving her medical license in the state of Colorado, she'd considered signing on with Doctors without Borders and going to Africa to help the many people who had no access to health care.

Her father had reminded her of those in need closer to home. He'd helped her apply for grants and had offered to fund her work, helping the people of their home state.

Staci found the work rewarding and the people happy to get any medical help, having gone without for most of their lives.

As she documented her patients in Glory Valley, she was seeing a trend that surprised and worried her.

She climbed into her SUV. Elizabeth slipped into the passenger seat beside her, pulling in the hem of her homemade gingham dress before she closed her door.

"What do you know about the accident?" Staci asked.

"Only what Peter, Abraham Faulkner's son, had to say. A man fell in the mine and injured his leg. They're pulling him out as we speak. The sooner we get there, the better."

Stace went through her mind all the things that could happen with an injured leg, from deep lacerations, a torn ACL or Meniscus or broken bones.

As she drove the gravel road up to the Glory Valley mine, she asked, "Elizabeth, how long have the community members been in this valley?"

"Since our father's father's fathers settled here in the mid-1800s." Elizabeth's chin rose. "They named it Glory Valley because it was the closest they'd ever get to heaven this side of the grave."

"What about during the gold rush? Weren't there more people in the valley then?"

Elizabeth's lips thinned. "Yes, there was. A terrible

time it was for our people. They moved deeper into the foothills to escape the crime and debauchery the mining camps brought with them. When those people moved on, we reclaimed the town and the mine."

"Did your people intermarry with the miners?"

Elizabeth snorted. "No. Our fathers kept their women and children away from the camps. Only the men had contact with the miners for work and trade."

"I notice there aren't a lot of children."

"Many of the young women aren't able to conceive. If they do, they've had multiple miscarriages. Why, Mary Landers had five miscarriages before she birthed little David." Elizabeth smiled. "She was so happy to bring her little boy into the world after so much heartache."

David Landers had been one of Staci's first patients when she'd set up shop in the lodge.

The baby was fifteen months old now and still hadn't learned to walk. He was in the tenth percentile for growth among babies his age, and his lungs weren't very strong. His mother brought him in because he'd had a constant cough for over a month, and he struggled to breathe.

When Staci had recently examined the child, he'd barely responded to her shining a light in his eyes. She suspected the boy's vision was impaired. When she'd questioned the mother, she'd responded slowly as if she couldn't quite understand simple questions.

When she'd asked Mary how old she was, she'd smiled. "I'll be eighteen next month."

Eighteen, and she'd had five miscarriages before giving birth to a child who was now fifteen months old? How old had she been when she'd had the miscarriages? How old had she been when she'd married? Staci performed rough calculations in her head. "How old was Mary when she married?" she asked Elizabeth.

Elizabeth stared out the front windshield. "Sixteen." Her tone dared Staci to say something.

Staci held her tongue and drove up an incline to the wooden building at the front of the mine. Where she'd grown up, sixteen was still considered a child.

As she pulled to a stop, men poured out of the building, moving out of the way to allow Staci and Elizabeth a clear path.

Inside the building, a man led them to the back, where the wood structure butted up against the rocky side of the mountain.

Four men emerged from a tunnel carrying a stretcher with a man laid across it.

Staci rushed forward and checked the man's pulse. It was strong but racing. He was breathing, and his face contorted in pain.

"What's your name?" she asked.

"His name is Marcus." Cyrus Severson, Elizabeth's husband, appeared at her side.

"I'd like him to answer," she said. "What's your name?"

The injured man's eyes blinked open. "Marcus," he bit out and bared his teeth, his body tensing. "Jesus, it hurts."

She didn't have to ask which leg had been injured. Someone had cut through the fabric of his blue jeans all the way up to his thigh. The lower part of his leg was red, and there were abrasions on the skin.

Starting at the knee, Staci ran her fingers along the tibia, feeling for fractures.

Marcus moaned. When she moved lower, he grabbed her hand. "Stop."

"I'm sorry," she said. "I can feel the bone is misaligned."

"What does that mean?" Marcus said.

"It snapped. It needs to be realigned. We need to get you to a hospital with an X-ray machine to better assess the damage. An orthopedic surgeon should take a look at it. The best I can do is stabilize you until we can get a life flight in to airlift you out."

The man's hand tightened around her wrist. "No."

"No, what?" she frowned. "No, you don't want to be flown out? We can call for an ambulance."

"No. Not leaving," Marcus said. "I'll be fine," he said through gritted teeth, his gaze on Cyrus Severson, not Staci.

29

"You need to be in a hospital where they can see where it's fractured. There might be more breaks I can't feel or bone fragments that need to be cleaned up."

"He stays," Cyrus said, his tone final.

Staci didn't give up easily, not where a patient's welfare was concerned. "This man should see a specialist. His bone is fractured. If it's not set correctly, his leg won't heal correctly. He might have a limp for the rest of his life."

Marcus stared into Cyrus's eyes, sweat beading on his forehead in the cool mountain air. "Not going."

Cyrus crossed his arms over his chest and met Staci's glare. "You're a doctor. You can set the bone."

How could she get through to these people? "If I set the bone, I could do it wrong. Marcus needs a specialist."

"All he has here is you," Cyrus said. "Set the bone."

She stared at Marcus. The man was at least six feet tall and weighed nearly two hundred pounds. Her mind went to the videos she'd studied about leg bones and tibia fractures and what to do when you were in an austere environment performing emergency medicine. "I don't even know if I'm strong enough to do it by myself. I've only seen it done. I've never performed the procedure."

"Tell us what to do," Cyrus said. "We can help."

Staci riffled through her bag. "I don't have the kind of pain medication to help him through this. I'm sorry," she said to Marcus. "It's going to hurt like hell."

"Just do it," he bit out.

She nodded toward Cyrus. "Hold onto his ankle. When I say pull, slowly pull the leg." She pointed to another man. "What's your name?"

The man stood taller. "Ezekiel, ma'am."

"You will hold Marcus beneath the armpits. When I say pull, you will hold on tight. Don't let him slip off the stretcher."

Once again, she smoothed her hands over his shinbone and felt for the break. Then she wrapped her hands around his leg on either side of the break. With a nod, she said, "Pull. Gently."

While Ezekiel held Marcus steady, Cyrus leaned back, holding onto the injured man's ankle.

Marcus screamed.

Staci did her best to realign the two ends of the break, and then said, "Okay, ease off."

Marcus sat halfway up, then blacked out and fell back against the stretcher.

Staci wiped the sweat from her brow and stood straight. "He'll need a splint to immobilize that leg while it mends. He'll have to stay off of it for at least four weeks, maybe longer. He can use crutches to get around, but he can't put weight on it while the bone is fusing."

Now that the one was set, Staci reached into her bag for gauze and alcohol to clean the abrasions.

Elizabeth touched her arm. "I can take over from here. I've done this before. You can go back to the lodge now."

Stace frowned. "I'm staying until my patient is stabilized."

Cyrus shook his head. "That won't be necessary. We'll get him home. Elizabeth can fix him up with a splint, and we'll get him comfortable until he's mended."

By then, Marcus was coming around.

Staci pulled a bottle of pain medication from her bag. "You'll need these for a couple of days to manage the pain." She gave him the directions and handed the bottle to Elizabeth. "You'll see that these make it home with him?"

She nodded and tucked the pills into the pocket of her dress.

Cyrus tipped his head toward Ezekiel. "Please show the good doctor back to her vehicle."

Anger flared in Staci's chest. "I know where my car is. I don't need someone to escort me there. I want to stay with my patient until I know he's going to be okay. He could go into shock."

"Elizabeth is capable of taking care of a person in shock. She has many years of experience." Cyrus met Ezekiel's gaze and lifted his chin.

"Come, Dr. Miller," Ezekiel said. "We need to get moving before it gets dark. And they need to get Marcus off the mountain and to his quarters so he can settle in with the medicine you gave him." Ezekiel's grip tightened on Staci's arm, and he more or less dragged her to her SUV.

Finally, she dug in her heels and yanked her arm loose. "What's wrong with you people? That man was seriously injured. He needs a hospital."

"The hospital is too far away. And we don't do things that way in the valley."

"Well, maybe you should." Staci climbed into her SUV and sat for a moment, watching as Elizabeth and the men wrapped a blanket around Marcus, tucking it beneath him on the stretcher. The men lifted the stretcher and loaded Marcus into the bed of a truck.

Elizabeth had yet to set the splint. If he traveled that way down the mountain, the bone could separate again. Not to mention the amount of pain Marcus would suffer through bumping along the rutted track.

Ezekiel knocked on her window. "Move along, Dr. Miller."

She started the engine and, against her better judgment, drove back down the mountain to the little town, parking in front of the lodge.

She expected the mountain people to be a little resistant to some forms of medical care, but Marcus really needed better care than she could give him in Glory Valley.

Staci grabbed her bag, still angry at the way Cyrus

ELLE JAMES

and Ezekiel had pretty much shut her down. And she was disappointed Elizabeth hadn't come to her defense. The woman was the community matriarch.

All the women, and most of the men, came to Elizabeth for advice or direction on how to get things done. If she was on board with Staci, they'd win over the men.

But she hadn't sided with the only medical doctor within a two-hour radius of driving.

Frustrated, tired and concerned, she entered the lodge and went up to her bedroom, where she dropped her bag. Then she crossed the hallway to the bathroom and washed her hands and face. She was still mad and needed to talk with someone. Her cell-phone hadn't worked since she'd crossed the pass to get into the valley. The lodge had a landline in the downstairs sitting room. She'd called her father from there when she'd arrived, and then again, the previous weekend to let him know she was doing well.

Maybe talking with him would bring her back from the ledge.

Stace left the bathroom, descended the stairs and entered the sitting room with its brown leather sofa and chairs and the massive stone fireplace with freshly stacked logs in the grate.

She'd enjoyed sitting in front of that fireplace several nights reading journals she'd brought with her.

Ruth Davis, the tiny, thin seventy-six-year-old manager of the lodge, entered the room from the direction of the dining room and kitchen. "Oh, Dr. Miller. Dinner is on a plate keeping warm in the oven. It's meatloaf, mashed potatoes and green beans. Would you like me to bring it in here for you to enjoy by the fire? I could light the fire for you if you like."

"Thank you, Mrs. Davis." Staci smiled. "I'll eat in the kitchen. I wanted to make a call first before it gets too late."

"Please. Help yourself." She crossed to take a seat in one of the leather chairs.

Staci stared at the woman, willing her to get up and go dust something in another room.

Ruth's gaze met hers. "Don't let me hold you up. Go on, make your call. You're not going to bother me." She reached into a basket beside the chair and pulled out knitting needles and a skein of colorful yarn. As she wrapped her fingers around the yarn, she shot a glance toward Staci and frowned. "Did you change your mind about that call?"

"Actually, yes." She hesitated to tell the woman she didn't want to talk while someone in the room was listening. "I'll wait."

"Okay." Ruth knitted several rows of the bright orange and red and yellow yarn. After a couple of minutes, she set the yarn aside and pushed to her feet. "I think I'll make some popcorn. Would you like some?"

"Thank you. But I think I'll eat dinner first." Staci left the sitting room, crossed through the dining area and pushed through the swinging door into the kitchen.

The plate covered in foil was warm in the oven.

Staci pulled it out, peeled back the foil and placed it on the kitchen table. After finding a fork and pouring a glass of tea, she sat at the table and ate the food provided, her mind going over everything that had happened at the mine.

She hadn't missed the way Marcus had met Cyrus's glance several times, as if he wanted Cyrus to know he didn't plan on leaving the valley. Had there been fear in his eyes? Or was she reading too much into their wordless exchange?

It hadn't taken Staci two weeks to know Cyrus was the head of the Glory Valley community. The people turned to him as much or more than they sought Elizabeth for help or guidance.

Because of the one winding, narrow road through the pass, they were basically isolated. Cut off from the rest of the world.

From her conversations with Elizabeth, she'd gathered that there were few visitors to Glory Valley. The lodge was rarely full. An occasional hunter would get lost in the mountains and find his way into town. Sometimes, hikers or mountain climbers made their way into the valley. They didn't stay long and usually disappeared back into the mountains.

Cyrus and some of the other men made a monthly supply run into the nearest town for staples and hardware. They used the money they made from the mine to purchase what they couldn't grow or make themselves. Or they sold woodwork or woven baskets to stores in the tourist towns.

They reminded Staci a little of the Amish or Mennonites in their desire to live off what they could produce themselves.

By the time she'd finished her meal, washed her plate and set it in the drainer to dry, her anger had subsided. But she was still concerned about Marcus and some of her other patients with physical abnormalities.

She was happy to find the sitting room empty, the basket with the yarn stowed next to the brown leather chair and Ruth nowhere in sight.

Quickly, while she was alone, she called her father on the antique rotary phone, the likes of which she hadn't seen since she'd visited her great grandmother when she'd been only six years old. She found it quaint and quirky…like Glory Valley.

"Hi, Daddy," she said.

"Hey, sweetheart, how's it going in the mountains? Is the altitude getting to you?"

She laughed. "Not since the first couple of days. I miss you."

"I miss you, too. When are you coming home?"

"I don't know. I feel like I have more work to do here in Glory Valley."

"You're a good doctor. I'm sure they're glad to have you there."

She sighed. "Sometimes, I feel like I've stepped back eighty to one hundred years in time. The town has some modern necessities, like running water and electricity, but then I go out to a few outlying homes, and it's like a different world. Dirt floors, outhouses and buckets in a well for water."

"Baby, come home. Your room is just as you left it when you went off to college. I haven't had the heart to change the way your mother decorated it."

He didn't add the statement she was thinking.

Before she died.

Her mother had passed away from Stage 4 breast cancer during Staci's junior year in high school. Heaven had gained the sweetest angel when Margaret Miller had left her husband and daughter behind.

If Staci had been on the fence about what she'd wanted to be when she grew up, her mother's death had solidified her determination to pursue a career in medicine.

"After the day I had, home sounds wonderful."

"Tell me about it."

She told him about her office in a supply closet and how Elizabeth Severson, the community matriarch and midwife, had assigned herself as the doctor's personal assistant. "She's with me for every patient. I can't tell if she thinks she has to interpret for me or whether she's protecting her people from the outsider."

"Is she kind?" her father asked.

Staci tipped her head to the side and thought about that. "I wouldn't say she's out-and-out kind, but she is concerned about her valley and the people in it. I think she's a little displaced by me and that I might be a threat to her standing." Staci laughed. "Sometimes, I overthink things."

"Most of the time, your instincts are right," her father said softly.

"Tonight, I had a standoff with her and her husband over what medical care a patient needed. He had a pretty badly broken leg. I told them I'd get him stabilized until they could call in a helicopter to airlift him out of there. You'd have thought I'd suggested he jump off a cliff."

Her father chuckled. "Not everyone is comfortable flying."

"I took that into account and suggested taking him in an ambulance to the nearest hospital, which happens to be more than two hours away."

"I take it they weren't keen on that idea either."

"No. They said I was the doctor. I should set the bone." Staci pulled the elastic band that held her hair back in a ponytail and shook it out.

"And did you?" he asked.

"With help from a couple of the men, yes." She frowned. "And as soon as we set the bone, they hustled me off the mountain and told me they'd take care of the rest. The way they acted…was weird. It was as if the patient was afraid of crossing the community leader or something. I wanted to stay and make sure he was stable, but they insisted they could handle it from there and sent me back down the mountain."

"Sounds kind of peculiar to me," her father said. "Is there something they don't want you to see?"

Were they hiding something? Staci asked herself.

"And these people haven't had any proper medical care. They rely on midwives, including the leader's wife, Elizabeth, who is my self-elected right hand and shadow. And they have no medical records. I've documented each of my cases, and I'm seeing a trend."

Staci glanced around the sitting room and peered into the darkened dining room. Ruth was nowhere to be seen.

Lowering her voice, she continued. "There are few children for a community of over two hundred people."

"Are they older? Have the young people moved on to the cities?"

"No. They're born, live and die in Glory Valley. I don't think anyone has left for greener pastures since the town was established. In a small community like this, it could cause problems among the population."

"How so?"

She described baby David and his mother. "But that's not all. There were other children with different abnormalities. One little girl had a misshapen face. There were a couple of boys with club feet. Elizabeth mentioned they'd had a lot of miscarriages among the young women."

"Do you think there are some toxins in the water?"

That had been one theory she'd researched, but she'd come around to another, equally disturbing. "I think the abnormalities in the children are from inbreeding."

"Seriously?"

"They seem quite proud that their families have been born, live and die here in Glory Valley."

"And the children are paying for that way of thinking. That's a shame. Is there anything you can do about it?"

"I'm not sure. Oh, and the girls marry young. I'm guessing around sixteen."

"Are you seeing any signs of abuse?" her father asked.

'Not so far, but then I haven't seen every member of the community." Her thoughts went back to Marcus and the look he'd given Cyrus. And then there was the callous way they'd loaded him up in a

41

truck. It would have been sheer torture riding down the mountain with a broken leg bumping along in the bed of that pickup.

"Sweetheart," her father said, "I'm not comfortable with you being out there by yourself."

Up until that day, Staci hadn't had any qualms about working in Glory Valley. "I'm okay," she said. "If the conditions continue to bother me, I'll pack up and head home."

"I wish you'd head home now," her father said.

"Really, Dad. I'm fine."

"Humor your old man and call me every day. I need that proof of life to satisfy the worrier in me."

Staci chuckled. "Okay. If it will make you feel better, I'll call again tomorrow evening."

"Thank you. I know you're a grown woman, and you have to live your own life, but you're also the only family I have," he said. "And there's always my purely selfish motive. I need to make sure you're still around to take care of me in my old age."

"You know I will. I love you to the moon and back."

"I love you more. Talk to you tomorrow night. And, Staci," her father's voice hardened, "if you feel at all weird, leave immediately."

"I will, Dad. Until tomorrow."

Her father ended the call.

She held onto the phone a little longer, a smile pulling at the corners of her mouth. When she started to set the phone on its cradle, she heard another click as if someone else was hanging up.

Then she recalled that another old phone hung on the wall in the kitchen.

Staci set the phone on the cradle, stood and walked softly across the sitting room, through the dining room and pushed the swinging door into the kitchen.

Expecting to maybe see Ruth, Staci stopped short and pressed a hand to her chest.

Ruth Davis stood beside Elizabeth. Cyrus stood beside his wife. Ezekiel, the man she'd met at the mine, stood on the other side of Ruth.

"Dr. Miller," Cyrus said, "Ezekiel's wife, Ruth, has brought it to our attention that we might have a problem."

A chill of apprehension slithered down the back of her neck. "Do I need my bag? Is someone sick or injured?" Feeling the fight or flight instinct kicking in, she turned to leave the kitchen. "I'll just get my bag."

Staci didn't make it out of the kitchen before a big hand closed around her upper arm and brought her to a sudden stop. She glanced back to discover Ezekiel holding onto her.

"I'll get your bag," Elizabeth said and pushed past Staci.

"Where are we going?" Staci asked, her gut telling her she wouldn't like the answer.

"You'll see when we get there," Cyrus responded.

The firm set of his face and the almost zealous gleam in his eyes made Staci take a risk.

"If it's all the same to you, I'd rather not go." She jabbed her elbow into Ezekiel's gut.

When his fingers loosened on Staci's arm, she dove through the swinging door and ran for the front entrance.

Elizabeth blocked the lodge door.

Staci spun and started up the stairs. She only made it up one riser when a hand caught in her hair and yanked her backward. Then a needle jabbed into her arm.

She glanced around at the faces of Cyrus, Ezekiel, Ruth and Elizabeth. "What have you done?" Staci demanded, and then her world went black.

CHAPTER 3

COLE HAD no idea what he was doing or what he was supposed to do. He'd walked into the basement headquarters of the Brotherhood Protectors' Colorado office in the lodge at Lost Valley Ranch with misgivings about the job he'd accepted.

He'd received no training, no cheat sheets and no guidance concerning what a protector actually did. The only explanation he'd received was from Jake. "You do whatever it takes to make a difference."

Was Jake kidding? What exactly did that mean? It sure wasn't helping with his first assignment.

Jake had said he'd received a call late the night before from Richard Miller, a wealthy man in Denver. He'd gotten information about the Brotherhood Protectors from Gunny Tate, an old friend and the man who owned the Lost Valley Ranch where he and his daughter had vacationed years before.

Miller wanted to hire one of the Brotherhood Protectors to find out why his daughter hadn't called him the night before and to make sure she was all right.

When Jake approached and immediately informed him of his first assignment, Cole had fought to keep from telling his new boss he really didn't want to get involved.

Cole snorted. Not that Jake would let him off the hook. Once committed, he couldn't go back.

Two and a half hours later, Cole drove through a mountain pass, following a narrow road down into a beautiful hidden valley. He had orders to go in undercover and see if the man's daughter was all right. If she was, he could connect with her and ask her if she needed anything in the way of support or protection.

Most likely, she'd think he was crazy and send him on his way. Hopefully, after he told her that her father was concerned, she would humor the old man and give him a call.

His cover was that he was a hiker and mountain climber interested in exploring the valley and the surrounding peaks. From what the woman's father had indicated, the valley wasn't well known or traveled. The people were a little backward, and his daughter, a doctor, had gone there to offer free medical care to their underserved population.

Cole had stuffed a backpack with MREs he had

left over from deployments, an extreme cold-weather sleeping bag, a lightweight tent, his camelback canteen, extra socks, clothes, a compass and a knife. He'd also packed a handgun in case he ran into trouble of the two or four-legged kind.

He'd had Thorn drive him through the pass and drop him off a couple of miles short of the floor of the valley. He'd hike in from there. Thorn would return in two days to the drop-off point. If Cole wasn't there, he'd assume that he'd run into trouble and would send in the rest of the team to bail him out.

Cole was ninety-nine percent convinced the daughter had forgotten to call, and her father had overreacted. That was okay with Cole. The job was getting him out of Colorado Springs and his haunted memories of his wife and son and the friend who shouldn't have died so soon.

People, including his therapist at the VA, had tried to tell him it just wasn't his time to die. There was a reason he was still alive...a purpose for his existence. He just had to find it.

Checking up on a rich man's daughter wasn't necessarily the purpose he'd had in mind. But it was a job, and he could be outside instead of stuck behind a desk selling insurance or used cars, which seemed like the only jobs he could land with his resume stacked with combat skills and wartime deployments.

As he pulled to a stop at the coordinates on the map for their drop-off point, Thorn asked, "You going to be all right?"

Cole shrugged. "Sure. How hard can it be to find a female doctor in a small town in the mountains?"

Thorn laughed. "Dude, you're tempting Murphy's Law with a statement like that. I think you just jinxed yourself. Now, whatever can go wrong will."

"I don't believe in luck or jinxes. This will be a slam dunk. I'll get in, find Dr. Miller, get her to check in with her dad and be back here for extraction in two days." He pushed open the door to Thorn's truck and dropped down. He opened the back door and retrieved his backpack. "Two days," Cole said as he shrugged into his backpack. With a wave, he set off down the road that twisted back and forth on the steep descent into Glory Valley.

The midday sun shone directly down on him, warming him in the cool of the mountain air. The air was thin at twelve thousand feet elevation, requiring more effort to breathe. With mountains on all sides, the valley probably didn't have as many hours of daylight as the eastern flatlands of Colorado.

Walking down the road took so much more time than it would have taken had Thorn driven him all the way in. He could already have been there, passed on Dr. Miller's message from her father and been back to the drop-off point for pickup.

As he descended into the valley, he took in the

terrain. There were stands of evergreen and aspen trees scattered all over the valley and halfway up the hills. From an overlook, he lifted his mini binoculars and scanned the scene below. A small town lay at the center of the bowl, with a main street and several cross streets. He could see what appeared to be a mine halfway up one of the mountains on the far side of the valley. Several farms situated on the outskirts of the town had lush patches of green growth and several greenhouses. Cattle and horses grazed in several fields.

The scene was idyllic, a place where Cole wouldn't mind living. Away from the noise and hustle of the city, where you could see the literal fruits of your labor in the food you could grow.

A glance at the sun tipping off its zenith pushed Cole on his way to reach the bottom well before the sun slipped behind the peaks.

He'd almost made it to the floor of the valley when he heard the sound of bleating animals. He searched for the source and spotted a herd of goats moving through a stand of trees into an open field. A teenage boy carrying a long stick walked behind them, trying to keep them moving and together.

When the boy spotted Cole, his eyes rounded, and he came to a complete stop.

Cole raised a hand in greeting. "Hey, got a minute?"

For a moment, Cole thought the boy might ignore

him and continue along his way, guiding the goats to what appeared to be a barnyard to the west of where they stood.

Cole walked over to the teen. "Is there a hotel or lodge in this town?"

The boy's gaze shot around as if looking to see if anyone was watching. He finally met Cole's glance. "No. You shouldn't stop here. There's nothing interesting to see in the valley."

"Oh, I don't know. Those peaks are calling to me." He grinned. "I like to climb peaks like those. Each is different...a challenge." His eyes narrowed, and his lips twisted. "There's seriously no place to stay here? I'd hate to have to walk back up that long-ass road tonight. Coming down wasn't so bad, but going up will take a lot longer."

The boy shook his head. "Seriously, you should go back to where you belong." He started to walk away.

"Hey, what's your name?"

The boy murmured something under his breath that sounded like Dalton Handler.

"Say again?" Cole tipped his head to the side.

The teen sighed. "They call me Joshua."

"Joshua, nice to meet you. Your parents live around here?"

A shadow passed over his eyes, and he glanced away. "My dad."

"Is he home?"

The boy shook his head. "No. And I have to go."

The goats had scattered, requiring Joshua to bring them back together. Once he had them moving in the right direction again, he glanced back. "Do yourself a favor. Don't stop here." He herded the goats through a stand of aspens to a field beyond the trees, glancing back as if checking to see if Cole would heed his words.

"Well, that wasn't strange at all," Cole muttered. He hadn't even made it into town, and a kid had already made it a point to tell him to leave.

So, the townspeople weren't all too friendly. He'd try to make this effort short and sweet.

The teen had disappeared with his herd of goats.

Cole continued to follow the road into the town at the center of Glory Valley.

The first structure he encountered on the left was a two-story building with the words Glory Valley Lodge written on a sign above the windows.

With a shake of his head, Cole entered the building and headed for the reception desk.

No one stood behind it.

Cole glanced around, searching for the clerk.

"Can I help you?" a woman said from behind him.

He turned. "Do you have a room available?"

She slipped behind the counter and checked in an old-fashioned registration book before nodding. "We might. How many nights will you be staying?"

"Maybe two," he said, sliding the backpack from his shoulders to rest on the floor.

"I'll have to check and get back with you in thirty minutes. In the meantime, my name is Ruth. If you need anything else, just let me know."

Why it would take thirty minutes to know if she had a room was beyond Cole's imagination. Either she knew or she didn't. Since it was the only option in town, he was stuck with her hesitancy. "Actually, could I leave my backpack here until you decide?"

Ruth's brow wrinkled. "I suppose you could leave it behind the desk here." She pointed to the floor beside her.

"Thanks." He dropped his backpack behind the desk and headed back outside. He wouldn't find the good doctor if he didn't get out and look. But where did he start?

Cole stepped back inside and approached the reception desk. "Excuse me, ma'am."

Ruth set an old-fashioned phone on its cradle and spun to face him, her cheeks turning a light pink. "Yes, my apologies. I sometimes get caught up in my work. How can I help you?"

He held up his thumb. "Got a splinter in my thumb. I don't suppose there's a doctor in this town?" He held his breath, praying he'd get his task complete before nightfall.

"I'll get her." Ruth left her post and stepped out the front door.

Cole waited, praying Ruth would come through and bring Dr. Miller back with her. He'd pretend he had a splinter. She'd try to fish it out, and he'd let her know her father was worried about her.

Easy.

He just had to get her alone in case she was working under duress.

Ruth returned with a woman who couldn't be Dr. Staci Miller. She was older and wore a handmade dress and apron, like a throwback to the 1930s.

"Ruth says you have a splinter that needs to come out?" the woman said. "I'm Elizabeth Severson."

He smiled. "Are you the doctor?"

She shook her head. "I'm not a doctor, but I am the closest thing we have in the valley. I'm a midwife with plenty of experience with splinters, scrapes and birthing babies." She held out her hand. "Let me see."

He placed his hand in hers and pointed to his thumb. "It's there. You can't see it, but I can feel it."

She stared down at it. "How long have you had it?"

"A week or so," he lied. Apparently, this wellness check on the doctor wasn't going to be quite the slam-dunk he'd anticipated. Not with this woman claiming she was the closest thing to a doctor in the valley.

He was in the right valley, wasn't he?

She stared down at his thumb, turning it in different directions. "I don't see anything."

"I feel it."

"Come with me." Still holding his hand, she led

him down a hallway to a door at the end and pushed it open. It appeared to be a small storage closet with a desk shoved against the wall. The desk was empty, except for a laptop pushed to the far corner. The laptop seemed incongruous to the lost-in-time feel of the people he'd met and the age of the few vehicles he'd seen parked along the street.

Elizabeth turned to a shelf on the wall behind the door. She retrieved a gauze pad, a bottle of rubbing alcohol and a sewing needle. She poured alcohol on the gauze, swiped the needle through the alcohol and used the gauze to wipe his thumb.

Her movements reminded him of all the times his mother had picked splinters out of his hands or cleaned scrapes and cuts from his many adventures in the woods. It didn't take a medical degree for that kind of nursing.

With the tip of the needle, she poked through the skin on his thumb, shaking her head. "Still don't see anything," she said. "How did you get the splinter?"

He shrugged. "I ran my hand over a piece of wood I was cutting in my garage before I'd sanded the rough edges. I didn't think much of it at the time."

She poked again, digging a little deeper.

The needle struck a nerve, sending a sharp pain through his hand. "Ouch." He jerked his hand back. "I think you got it," he said and put his hand behind his back. "Thanks." He looked around the little office where he and the midwife could barely stand together. "Is this all the medical support you have here?"

"It's all we need," Elizabeth said, turning to place the bottle of alcohol on the shelf.

"What happens when you have a medical emergency? Do you call for a helicopter or something?"

"The midwives handle most everything," she said.

The *most* part troubled him. In his briefing with Jake and Dr. Miller's father tapped in on teleconference, he'd learned the good doctor had expressed concern over a patient they'd refused to take to a hospital for a broken leg. She'd also talked about children with abnormalities associated with inbreeding.

Cole had done some surfing on the web to look up some of those abnormalities, which included misshapen faces, developmental delays and schizophrenia. The people in the valley were isolated by their location and preferred to keep to themselves, she'd said, which would account for inbreeding in a population with a limited gene pool.

Elizabeth turned with a smile that didn't quite seem to reach her eyes. "If that's all, I guess you'll be going?"

Cole stepped out into the hall. "Actually, I thought I might stay a few days. I love hiking and climbing mountains, and the surrounding peaks appeal to me." He glanced down the hallway toward the reception desk. "I'm waiting to hear from Ruth if they have a vacancy here at the lodge."

Elizabeth's lips tightened. "I think I heard Ruth say they were booked."

"I'll doublecheck with Ruth to see if she found a room. If she can't put me up, that's okay." He dipped his head. "I have a tent."

"It gets cold here at night. You might want to stay somewhere at a lower altitude."

He grinned. She wasn't getting rid of him that easily. "Got that covered with my cold-weather sleeping bag." Cole forced a smile. "I've done this before."

The woman was definitely trying to get him to leave. Why? And where was the doctor? Her father said she'd been working in the town for two weeks.

His gaze went to the laptop on the desk in the little room. "How do you like your laptop? I have one like it. Does your battery last long enough? Mine only lasts between ten and twelve hours."

Elizabeth's gaze followed his to the laptop lying on the desk. "I get at least that many hours out of it." She pulled the door closed. "Now, if you'll excuse me…"

"Do I owe you for helping me with the splinter?"

She shook her head. "No. That won't be necessary."

A door slammed in the front of the lodge, and a voice called out, "Dr. Miller! Dr. Miller!" A young woman, who couldn't be much more than a child, appeared at the end of the hallway carrying a baby.

"Elizabeth, where's Dr. Miller? The dog ate the syringe the doctor gave me for David's medicine. I can't get him to take it any other way. Does she have a spare?"

Elizabeth shot a sideways glance at Cole before she turned and reentered the closet office then dug into a box on the shelf. She handed the woman the syringe.

"Oh, thank you. I'll be careful not to let the dog eat this one." She hiked the baby on her hip and smiled up at Cole. "Oh, I don't know you. You must be a stranger."

Cole nodded. "Hi, I'm Cole, and yes, I'm new in town."

"I'm Mary," the girl said and smiled down at her baby. "This is David. Say hi to the nice man," she cooed at the baby."

David stared straight ahead without blinking. His head seemed overly large, even for a baby, and his body was tiny, his limbs thin. He coughed, the sound more like a gurgle. Cole's heart went out to the kid. He didn't look well, and his mother wasn't much more than a kid herself.

"Hi, David," Cole reached out to touch the little guy's hand.

David wrapped his little fingers around Cole's pinky. A flood of emotions swept over Cole. He remembered when he'd gotten home from deployment when Tyler had already been three months old.

He'd been a happy, healthy little boy, smiling, cooing and giggling. He'd gripped Cole's finger much like David was now.

Cole's heart constricted. He wanted to reach out and take little David in his arms and hold him tight. He hadn't gotten to hold his Tyler nearly enough before he'd been taken away from him.

"Mary, take David home. He doesn't need to be out and about with that cough." Elizabeth's tone was one of command.

Mary nodded meekly, tossed a smile at Cole and said, "It was nice meeting you. We don't get many visitors around here."

"Nice meeting you, Mary," Cole managed to say past the lump in his throat. "Take care of that baby."

"I will," she said and hurried back the way she'd come.

Cole turned to Elizabeth.

She stood unshakable, with her chin raised as if daring him to say something.

He wanted to call the woman out on lying about there not being a doctor in town. Instead, he gave her a brief nod and a smile. "Thanks again, Ms. Elizabeth."

She dipped her head once, turned and marched down the hallway to the front entrance of the lodge. A door opened and slammed shut. Cole followed more slowly, stopping when he spotted Ruth, standing at the picture window looking out over Main Street.

Cole glanced out the window to see what had captured her attention.

Elizabeth stood in the street talking with two men. As one, the men looked toward the lodge.

Ruth backed up and turned away. When she spotted Cole, her face flushed a bright pink. "Can I help you?" She moved across the room, away from the window.

Cole's gaze swung back to the window where the two men and Elizabeth seemed to be in an intense conversation. The men kept looking toward the lodge, their eyes narrowed.

Oh, yeah, something was up, and his assignment just got more interesting. He turned back to Ruth with a friendly grin. "Did you find a room for the next couple of nights?"

She wrung her hands, her gaze darting toward the front window. "I don't know...let me...check."

"The town doesn't get many visitors, does it?"

Ruth shook her head. "But we've been doing... renovations on some of the rooms. I'll have to make sure one is ready. If you'd like to have a seat, I'll be right back." She motioned for him to take a seat in the sitting room, away from the front window.

Cole sat in the brown leather chair she'd indicated.

Ruth scurried out of the room.

Once she was out of sight, Cole stood and moved toward the window.

The two men and Elizabeth were still in discussion when Ruth appeared from around the side of the building. She joined the three and spoke quickly, looking back at the lodge.

Cole shook his head. He didn't like that they seemed to be discussing what to do with him.

When Ruth turned to go back around the building again, Cole returned to the brown leather chair and sat.

Ruth appeared a minute later. "Yes. I do have a room for you. If you'll follow me, I'll show you where it is."

He found it even more interesting that Ruth had to get permission from the two men and Elizabeth to rent a room to him. He was quickly learning the pecking order in Glory Valley. It appeared Elizabeth was the top hen, and one, or both, of the men she'd been talking with was the top rooster.

The question still outstanding was: where were they hiding the good Dr. Miller?

"Dinner will be ready at six," Ruth said.

After stowing his gear, Cole left the lodge and walked the length of Main Street. The people he passed waved politely but didn't stop to talk to him.

He turned down one of the side roads that led out of town into the wooded foothills of one of the surrounding peaks. A tenth of a mile past the last house was a gated cemetery surrounded by lodgepole pines. He paused to lean on the fence and study the names on the headstones. There were only about twenty different surnames and far too many tiny stones for children.

Dr. Miller was probably right; this community could be suffering from inbreeding, which would affect them physically and mentally.

No one was going to tell him where they'd taken Dr. Miller. If they were holding her hostage, he had to push them into revealing where she was. The alternative was to convince them to take him hostage as well and hope they would take him where they were holding her. From there, he'd figure his way out with the doc.

"You shouldn't have come," a voice said softly from the shadow of a nearby tree.

Cole shot a glance in that direction.

A teenage girl sat with her back to the tree, a straw in her mouth, looking bored, like most teens.

"Why?" he asked.

"Lone man. Stranger in town." She shrugged. "Never ends well."

He chuckled. "I'll need a little more to go on."

"Yeah, well, that's all I have. The rest will be up to you. You should leave before it's too late." Her gaze went past him, and she shook her head. "Speak of the devils. It's already too late." She stood, swung up into the tree and disappeared into the foliage.

Cole turned to see four men headed his way. The two who had been talking to Elizabeth out in front of the lodge and two others, even bigger.

He faced them with a smile. "Is this the town welcoming committee?"

"Not hardly," said the man in the lead with thick brown hair and brown eyes. "We heard you were looking for a place to stay for a few days and thought we'd help you out."

"Thanks, but I have a place at the lodge."

"Well, that's just it; you're no longer staying at the lodge. We canceled your reservation and moved you to other accommodations."

"That's real nice of you," Cole said, his fighting instincts on high alert. Eventually, he'd allow them to take him, but first, he wanted to inflict a little pain on these bastards. He prayed the doctor was where they would take him.

Bracing his legs, he got ready for the fight.

Suddenly, the man in the lead reached into his jacket and whipped out a gun.

"Crap," Cole murmured and flung himself to the side, two seconds too late.

Probes struck him in the side, and a shock of electricity ripped through him. Cole hit the ground, completely immobile. He could hear and see, but he couldn't move a single muscle.

Well, fuck.

CHAPTER 4

STACI WOKE to a pounding headache and a dry mouth. She lay on a hard, thin mattress in a dark room that smelled of damp earth and rock. She shivered in the chill air and sat up.

A muffled moan sounded from somewhere nearby.

"Hello?" she called out softly into the darkness.

Another moan sounded, a little louder.

"Hello?" Staci spoke a little louder. "Who's there?"

The moaning stopped.

"Where am I?" she asked the darkness.

"You're in...one of the mine tunnels...they converted into cells," a voice called out as if straining against something.

Staci suspected he was straining against pain. "Are you hurt?"

"Yes." The man's response was short and sharp.

"Do you have a name?"

"Marcus. Screw that."

"What?"

"My name is Mark Chandler. They made me use Marcus Simeon if I ran into anyone outside the valley. And you're the doctor who set my leg."

Staci gasped. "You're that Marcus?"

"Yes," he responded and groaned. "This leg hurts like hell."

"I'm so sorry," Staci said. "I'm Dr. Miller. I wish I could have done more for you."

"They weren't going to let you send me anywhere."

"They said they were taking you home to recuperate."

Mark snorted. "Now you know why they didn't want you to come."

"Did they at least give you the pain medication I left with Elizabeth?"

"Hell, no."

Anger burned deep in Staci's gut. "What are you, some kind of prisoner?"

"Yes."

"But you weren't chained or guarded by men carrying weapons."

"They have a much more useful weapon," he said, his tone flat and defeated.

"What is it?"

"My son."

"I don't understand."

"They have my son. They told me if I ever try to escape or tell anyone that we're being held hostage, they'll kill my boy."

Staci shook her head. "This can't be happening. On the surface, they appear to be normal folks, trying to eke out a living on the land."

Mark snorted. "Only they can't. They have to have money to sustain the community. That's where the mine comes in. And they need miners to dig for the rare metals that can be found in the Glory Hole Mine."

"How did you get here?" Staci asked.

"Oh, Jesus, my leg hurts." Mark moaned.

Staci didn't push for a response. A few moments passed in silence.

"As a present for my son's fifteenth birthday, I promised to take him hunting in Colorado," Marcus said. "We got lost in the woods and ended up crossing the mountain pass into Glory Valley." He laughed without humor. "We were so glad to see houses and people. We had no idea we were walking into a trap."

"It's so hard to believe that they are that diabolical," Staci said.

"Right? At first, they seemed so warm and friendly. They fed us, made sure we were comfortable in the lodge, and then I woke up here. I haven't seen my son since that night. It's been two months."

Staci's stomach clenched. "What's your son's name?"

"Dalton Chandler. He's a tall, skinny kid with a mop of brown hair and brown eyes like me. I meant to take him by for a haircut before our hunting trip, but I got too busy and never did. Have you seen him?"

Staci thought back over the young people she'd seen in town as she'd come and gone with Elizabeth by her side. At one point, she recalled a tall, thin young man out in a field with a herd of goats. She'd asked Elizabeth about the goats and what they did with them. She would never have guessed the goat herder was a hostage. They'd probably fed him the same line as they had his father. If he screwed up, his father would pay with his life. "I think I saw him out in a field with a herd of goats."

"Tall? Too skinny? Scraggly hair?" Mark asked, his voice desperate, lonely for his kid.

"It had to be him," Staci said. "There's only one other young man I've seen that even comes close. He's got short blond hair, and he's not as tall."

"How'd he look? Was he okay?" Mark asked.

"I only saw him from a distance. He appeared okay, physically."

"Thank you," Mark said.

A long silence stretched between them.

"Hey, Doc, will you do me a favor?" Mark asked softly in the darkness.

"If I can," Staci responded. She couldn't do much in her current state.

"If I don't make it out of here, will you make sure my boy goes to a good home? My wife passed away a year ago. Our parents are gone. It was just me and Dalton against the world. Tell him I'm sorry I failed him, and that I love him with all my heart."

Tears welled in Staci's eyes. She swallowed hard before she could answer. "You're going to make it out of here. *We're* going to make it out of here, and you'll take your son home where he belongs. With you."

"But if I don't...please. Will you do that for me? Promise?"

Her heart aching, Staci said, "I promise."

But she'd be damned if she let Mark die. She would find a way out of there and come back with help for Mark and his son.

She stood and felt her way around the cell. The back wall was the hard rock of the tunnel. The sides of her cell were concrete block walls. The front was a continuation of the concrete blocks up to a door made of iron bars. She stuck her hand through the bars and found a lock securing the door.

Without a key, a file or even a paper clip, she had no way of releasing the lock.

One by one, she tried to twist the bars on the gate. Someone had done a good job welding the metal. Each bar was securely in place.

Staci cocked her leg and kicked the bars several

times, hoping to shake them loose from the hinges. She only managed to hurt her foot.

"I've tried everything," Mark said. "The cells are pretty tight."

"Are there others who've been kidnapped by the valley people?"

"Yes. They're probably working the mine right now. They'll bring them back around six o'clock, feed us and then be back at six in the morning to start the day all over."

Staci stood frozen in horror at a secret that had been hiding in plain sight the entire two weeks she'd been in the valley. "Sweet Jesus, how many people have they detained?"

"There are four of us. We can barely keep up with the workload. I fully expect they'll want me back at work tomorrow. Because if I can't work, they have no use for me."

Staci pressed her hands to her cheeks. "What will they do with you?"

"Probably put me out of my misery. People shoot lame horses, don't they? To them, I'm nothing more than a horse."

"We can't let that happen." She grabbed the rails again and shook them. "How do they feed you?"

"They slide a flat cardboard box beneath the cell door."

Staci dropped to her haunches and felt for the gap

on the floor. If it was big enough, she might slide beneath it and get out that way.

The gap was barely three inches tall. Even if she could get her body through, her head would never make it.

She sat on the floor, trying to think. She scratched her fingernails across the floor. It was like the back wall, solid rock.

Her escape had to coincide with the twice-daily schedule of letting the prisoners in and out of their cells for work in the mine.

"They can't do all the work without me. We were already doing the work of two men each. They'll have to find another poor schmuck wandering into their valley. One who has few contacts on the outside who would worry when he doesn't show up."

"Who are the others?" Staci asked.

"Will Mathis, a thirty-two-year-old web designer, who liked to hike in the Rockies. Robert Bagley, a forty-two-year-old divorced salesman, who took a wrong turn and ended up in Glory Valley. Then there's the kid, twenty-one-years-old, Sean Keller, a bicyclist training for the world championship."

"Sean Keller?" Staci thought back to the news reporter talking about a nationally ranked bicycle champion who had gone missing in the mountains. "I can't believe nobody has looked here."

"They put on a good show for the authorities. Good

people who work hard don't abduct strangers to work in their mine. They made us take on biblical names. If we don't use them, they hit us with cattle prods."

"Bastards," Staci muttered.

"All I want is to go home with my son. All any of us wants is to go home."

Staci felt the same.

A metal door slammed open somewhere nearby, allowing a little light to filter into the darkness. The sound of grunts and curses echoed against the rock walls.

Staci strained to see what was happening.

Four men carried one struggling man and a flashlight between them. They passed Staci and stopped at the next cell.

"Shine the damned light this way," Cyrus Severson demanded as he pulled a ring of keys from his pocket, thumbed through several and then jammed one into the padlock. He twisted the key, and the lock released.

Cyrus stood back as the other men shoved the big guy into the cell.

"You should've hit him again with the taser," one man said, rubbing his jaw. "He kicked me in the chin."

Ezekiel snorted. "You'd think once would be enough."

"He came around too fast," said the guy rubbing his jaw.

"Doesn't matter. It's done," Cyrus said. "We'll put him to work tomorrow with the others."

"What are we going to do with Marcus?" Ezekiel asked.

"I'm thinking about it," Cyrus said.

"He won't be any good to us for several more weeks," Ezekiel pointed out.

Cyrus nodded. "Even then, he won't be doing any heavy-lifting without risking breaking the bone again. Waste of time and money keeping him here," Cyrus said. "But I'm still debating."

"If we get rid of him, what would we do with the boy?" Ezekiel asked.

"We could have him take over for his father," Cyrus said. "That would give him time to mend, and then we'd have both of them to work the mines."

Staci's blood boiled. She'd listened to their bullshit for long enough. "What you're doing is illegal," she called out. "Holding people against their will is not right. You won't get away with this."

Cyrus stepped up to her cell and sneered down at her. "Nobody knows about our existence here in Glory Valley, and we like it that way. It's been like this for as long as we can remember. It'll be like this for our children and our children's children. They don't know what they don't see."

"Yeah. It's only illegal if you get caught," Ezekiel said.

Cyrus shook his head. "It's illegal, but you only go to jail if you get caught."

Ezekiel nodded. "Right."

"It's not right to abduct people and use them to work your mine," Staci said. "Let us go."

Cyrus crossed his arms over his chest. "Can't. We don't have enough able-bodied men to produce the gold we need to sustain our people."

"Then you have to find another way." Staci gripped the metal bars. "Pay people to work the mine."

"If we pay people to work the mines, they'll move into our valley and bring their families and ideas with them. Then they'll want our women and tempt our men. We will not have outsiders intermarrying with our people. They'll taint our blood," Cyrus said.

"By isolating yourselves, you've already tainted your blood," Staci said. "You're damaging your genetics with inbreeding. You're killing the children of your future."

Cyrus shook his head. "The bottom line is that we can't let you go. You know too much. You'll have to stay."

"Drop it, Dr. Miller," Mark said.

"They have to let us go," Staci insisted.

Cyrus shook his. "No, we don't. No one will ever know you're here." He turned to Ezekiel. "Let's go."

The men left, taking the light with them, leaving Mark, Staci and the new guy in the dark.

"You're wasting your breath talking to them," Mark said. "They can only see what they want to see. They are absolutely convinced they're saving their people."

"But they can't keep us forever," Staci said.

"Dr. Miller, they're in too deep now. Once they kidnapped their first unlucky soul, they couldn't undo the damage. The only way they will let us go is if they kill us first and bury the bodies."

"Well, that's not an option." Staci kicked the barred gate again. "We just have to wait. We'll be missed. Someone will come looking."

"People get lost in the mountains all the time," Mark said. "I'm sure that's what my neighbors back home in Texas think. They might even think we've moved. I guess when the mortgage company comes to foreclose on our home, it'll look like we abandoned it."

"Mark, we're getting out of here," Staci said. "Hey, mister, are you okay?"

"Maybe," a voice sounded from the cell on the other side of Staci's.

"Which one of the guys are you?" she asked. "Will, Robert or Sean?"

"None of the above," he said. "Cole."

"Well, damn, they snagged another warm body to do their dirty work," Mark said.

"How did you end up in Glory Valley?" the woman asked.

"I came to find Dr. Miller." He laughed. "Mission accomplished."

His body tingled as the effects of the taser wore off. Little by little, he regained control of his muscles. While he'd lain on the hard rock floor, he'd listened as his captor told the doctor they would never let them go.

That guy would be sorely disappointed when Cole left with the doctor they were holding hostage. Once he had her safely away from Glory Valley, he'd come back to free the others.

"You came to find me?" Dr. Miller asked.

"Your father sent me. He wanted me to remind you to call him in case you forgot."

The doctor laughed. "I should've known my father would worry if I didn't call. He's a decent human and the best father a girl could hope for. Was that all you came to do? To remind me to call my father?"

"That's what I thought. Come to a pretty mountain town, remind a man's daughter to call her worried father and leave town the same day."

The doctor snorted. "So much for leaving the same day."

"Technically, I did," he said.

"But not on your own two feet," she reminded

him. "And you didn't make it back to wherever you came from. What's your name?"

"Bryce Coleman. My friends call me Cole."

"Well, Mr. Coleman, how do you propose getting us out of here?"

"I'm working on it," he said. "Give me a minute."

"Did they shoot you with a sedative to knock you out?"

Cole rubbed the spot where the taser probes had hit him. "Tased. Didn't see that coming."

"Yeah, the hometown welcome lures you in." Dr. Miller sighed. "We're waiting patiently for you to figure a way out of this mess. Please, Mr. Coleman, take your time."

"Cole. Mr. Coleman sounds so formal for someone you're sharing a jail with. What is this place?"

"Mining tunnel turned indentured servants' quarters," the man on the far side of the doctor's cell called out.

"It's so damned dark." Cole blinked as if he could eventually regain some night vision.

"You never quite get used to it. We go from this dark hole to the other side of the mine to work extracting ore. At least there, we have some light to work with. I'd give every cent in my savings to stand in the sunshine for fifteen minutes," Mark said. "I never realized how lucky I was to live in Texas where there's sunshine."

"And then you got stuck in this hell hole," the doc said. "Your son must be beside himself."

"Your son?" Cole asked. "Have they imprisoned your son as well?"

"In a way. They know he won't leave without me. And they threaten to harm him if I don't do what they say," Mark said.

Cole remembered the boy herding goats and how he'd acted strange, telling him his name. "Is his name Dalton?"

"Yes!" Mark said. "You've seen him?"

"I talked to him today. He was herding goats. Tall young man with brown hair?"

"That's him. He's okay?"

"Seemed to be. I saw no signs of abuse."

"It gives me hope," Mark said. "Except for this damned leg."

"What happened?"

"Broke it today. Dr. Miller set it."

"He needs to go to a hospital, get X-rays and have an orthopedic surgeon look at it," Dr. Miller said. "He might need pins to keep it in place until it heals properly."

"Then we need to get out of here," Cole said.

"I've tried. The bars are welded solid, and the lock isn't budging," the woman in the cell next to him said.

"Well, Doc, we'll have to think of something else."

Cole pushed to his feet, felt his way around his cell and stood with his hands on the bars until he was steady like his old self before being tased. He tested the bars by shaking them. Like the doc said, they were sturdy and welded solid. He tried lifting the gate to see if it would come off the hinges.

Nope.

Then he kicked the gate, hitting as close to the lock as he could get when he couldn't see in the dark. Other than making a loud noise, it didn't shake loose. Whoever had built the cells had done a good job, which was too bad for them.

"I take it you're not having any more luck than I did," she said.

"I haven't given up," Cole said. There was always a way out if you looked hard enough.

After exploring his cell again with his hands, he admitted he wasn't getting out by digging or breaking the bars. He'd have to find another way. And soon. Since they were in a tunnel inside a mountain, he was almost positive his implanted GPS device wouldn't send out a signal strong enough for Jake and his Brotherhood Protectors to find him. He'd have to get himself out of the mountain and take Dr. Miller with him.

CHAPTER 5

STACI SAT on the hard mattress that was maybe two inches thick at best and wrapped a coarse wool blanket around her shoulders. She pulled her knees up to her chest and tried to think warm thoughts.

Her heart went out to Mark, whose pain had to be making it hard for him to sleep. As soon as she could escape the tunnel and the valley, she would get help to free the prisoners.

Will, Robert and Sean were brought back to the tunnel not long after Cole was deposited in his cell. They occupied the cells on the far side of Mark. They were exhausted from working the long day in the mine.

Food was delivered on cardboard trays and shoved beneath the bottom of the gate. No utensils were provided, and the cups containing water were metal and couldn't be broken to make sharp knives out of them.

Staci was almost glad she couldn't see what she was eating or the condition of her cell. It was bad enough that the toilet facilities consisted of a bucket in the corner with no running water to wash with.

All she could hope was for a medical emergency in the community that would necessitate calling on the doctor. They'd have to take her out of the cell. It would give her the opportunity she needed to escape and find help.

"Are you asleep, Dr. Miller?" Cole called out quietly.

"No," she answered. "And please, call me Staci. Dr. Miller sounds too formal for this environment."

"Staci, you asked me why I came to Glory Valley. Why did you come?"

She didn't answer for a minute.

"You don't have to answer if you think it's none of my business," he said.

"No, it's not that," she said. "At first, I thought it was my altruistic way of giving back to a world that had given me so much. I had everything a girl could want growing up. A nice house, private schools, parents who loved me. Everything."

"Sounds like a perfect childhood," Cole commented.

Staci listened for the sarcasm or derision others might demonstrate because she'd had so much, and they might not have been so fortunate. Cole's words were stated as fact, without any sense of judgment in his tone or inflection.

She liked that.

"When my mother died, I learned the hard lesson that I couldn't have everything I wanted because my father couldn't buy my mother's life. No amount of money would cure her cancer. She died a few days short of my seventeenth birthday."

"I'm sorry," Cole said quietly.

"I knew I was privileged to have such a blessed life others envied. Instead of feeling guilty or ashamed of it, I made the best use of it and got an education that would allow me to give back to those who couldn't afford medical care or lived too far from a hospital to get there when they were sick.

"I thought I was doing it for my patients. It was, and it wasn't. I found that I was doing it for me. It made me feel good to help others. If it made them feel good, it made me feel even better. So no, I didn't come to help others because I'm altruistic. I did it because I'm selfish, and it makes me feel good to help others."

Cole chuckled. "That's messed up."

She frowned, and then her frown lifted, and she smiled into the darkness. "Yeah, it is a little messed up. I could never be a nun. I have too much pride, and I'm not at all selfless. And I like wine, and I want children someday. What about you? Why did you take a job to come find me? Were there no other jobs available that were more interesting?"

"Nothing that fit my training and skillset."

"And what kind of training and skillset would that be?"

"I recently left the Army."

Staci sat up straighter, wishing she'd gotten a better look at Cole when they'd dragged him into the tunnel. "Retired?"

"No, disillusioned."

"Explain?" she prompted.

"I was good at what I did as a Delta Force operator. We performed missions all over the world, whether it was rescuing American citizens or political prisoners or taking out dangerous terrorists. I liked being a part of something bigger than just me."

"I get that." Staci felt the medical profession was kind of like that. Though she wasn't taking out terrorists, she was rescuing lives, in a way.

"I was away sometimes three hundred and sixty-five days a year."

"That doesn't leave room for a life outside your work," Staci said.

"I had a wife and son," Cole said, his tone deep and sad.

"Had?" she asked softly.

"I was in Afghanistan on a deployment when my wife and son were killed in a traffic accident."

Her chest tightened. "I'm sorry. That had to be difficult."

"She was pregnant with our second child. The woman was a saint. She didn't complain about me being gone all the time. When I missed important milestones in our marriage or our son's childhood, she understood and made our time together even more special. When they died, I couldn't make up for lost time. I couldn't get those occasions back."

Staci had no words that could help Cole. He had to fight his own demons and come to forgive himself for not being there.

"With no one to go home to, I threw myself into my military job, volunteered for deployments and tried to forget everything I'd lost.

"I felt like I was handling it well, getting on with life."

"You were running away from your life," Staci said.

"That's right. I didn't realize that until my last mission. You'll get a kick out of this…We deployed to rescue a US citizen working with Doctors without Borders in Somalia."

Staci's lips twisted. "I take it that mission didn't go any better than this one has so far."

"I lost my best friend and battle buddy. His wife lost a husband, and her children lost their daddy that day. All I could think as he lay dying in my arms was, it should have been me."

"So, you left the military to find yourself," Staci said.

He didn't answer.

"I was engaged right out of med school."

"Congratulations," Cole said.

She laughed. "When he found out I wanted to work with the poor, he told me it wasn't going to work. He wanted me to work in Denver at one of the more prestigious clinics, working with wealthy clientele." She sighed. "He was right. We never would've worked."

"We should try to sleep," Cole said. "I'm sure they'll have lots of work for me tomorrow. I've never been in a mine before. It should be a learning experience."

Staci lay on her side on her mattress and closed her eyes. "So, what's the plan when we get out of here?"

"Get as far away from Glory Valley as possible. And when we get to a saner place, get the authorities involved and bring them back to free the others."

Staci yawned. "Sounds good. Let me know when you figure out how we'll make our escape."

"Will do."

"And Cole?" Staci opened her eyes in the dark.

"Yes, Staci."

"It wasn't your time to die. There's a reason you're still alive."

"And what reason is that?" he asked.

"To save me," she said and closed her eyes again.

"I haven't done that yet," he said.

"You will," she said and slipped into a deep sleep. Knowing she had someone there to help her escape also helped her keep the faith that it would happen, and she'd be back for Mark, his son and the others imprisoned in the tunnel.

COLE LAY for a long time thinking about Staci and her desire to give back to her state. She might have been born into privilege, but she wanted to make a difference and help others. Sitting in the dark, talking through the wall, had been strangely...nice. He felt like they'd opened up more about each other's lives than if they'd been sitting together bathed in light.

The women he'd talked with since his wife's death had only been interested in establishing a relationship. One date, and he was done. The thought of exposing his heart again made him turn and walk away every time. It had hurt too much to lose Lisa and Tyler.

With the doc, he didn't have to worry that she might expect more from him than to get him out of the mess she'd landed in. They weren't on a date; she wasn't in the market for a man, and he wasn't in the market for a woman. They were just two people filling the silence in the dark. It was nice. Comforting and unassuming.

Cole finally slept, only to be woken in what felt like was still the night. With the darkness so complete, he had no idea what time it was, just that the noise was deafening.

Someone banged metal against metal incessantly. "Get up! Time to work!"

A guard wearing a headlamp bent to shove a cardboard box containing food beneath his gate. When he straightened, he shined his light into Cole's eyes. "Eat fast or go hungry until dinner."

Cole rolled off the mattress and stood. In the limited glow of the man's headlamp filtering through the bars, he found the tray of food and scarfed it down with his hands. The tray contained scrambled eggs, bread and some kind of oatmeal. It wasn't horrible, and it would provide the strength he'd need to work in the mine.

Ten minutes after the food was delivered, the guard came back through with a couple of his friends and unlocked the cells of the men who would be working in the mine. Each guard carried a cattle prod. A couple had tasers hooked on their belts.

As they passed Staci's cell, she called out. "I'm strong. I could work just as hard as the men."

"You're the doctor," one of the guards said. "You'll do what doctors do."

"Not if I'm sitting in this cell," she said.

"They'll come for you," another man said. He was one of the men who'd been talking to Elizabeth in front of the lodge the day before.

"Ezekiel," Staci called out to the man. "This is crazy. You can't just kidnap people and force them to work for you."

"But we have," Ezekiel said.

"What's happening here isn't right," Staci said. "You're destroying people's lives."

"And if we don't, we destroy the lives of everyone in this community," Ezekiel said. "We care about the folks of Glory Valley."

"But your prisoners are people, too."

Cole could see the man sneer. "Not *our* people. They shouldn't have come to our valley. *You* shouldn't have come," Ezekiel bit out.

"When the men of this community are caught—and you will be—you'll all go to jail for a long time. What will happen to your people then?" Staci's voice was low, strong and unwavering.

Cole wanted to cheer for her. She wasn't backing down from these people. The woman was seriously independent and kick ass.

Ezekiel stared into the cell Staci occupied. "You're to stay here until someone needs a doctor." He moved on to Cole's cell and unlocked the door. "Move." He said, waving his cattle prod.

When Cole remained standing where he was, the

other man's eyes narrowed. "We can do this the easy way, or you can take it the hard way. Your choice."

Not in any hurry to be zapped with electricity from the cattle prod after being immobilized the day before by a taser, Cole raised his hands. "I'm coming." He wouldn't fight back until he reconned the lay of the land and maybe filched a tool he could use to break the lock.

As he stepped through the gate, the bastard tagged him with the tip of the cattle prod, sending a jolt of electricity through him.

Cole jumped back and cursed. He glared at the man and brought up his fists, ready to punch him in the throat. "What the hell?"

"You needed to know we mean business." Ezekiel gave him a narrow-eyed glare. "Don't fuck up."

Still burning inside from the shock, Cole kept his hands balled into fists, and his muscles bunched, ready to take down the man and break his torture toy into a million pieces.

"You want some more?" Ezekiel took a step toward Cole.

"Need a hand back there, EZ?" A flashlight shone toward the two men in a stand-off.

Knowing the other men with cattle prods would come down on him if he made a move on Ezekiel, Cole forced himself to drop his arms to his sides. He wouldn't get far in the tunnel without a weapon, and he needed to get out long enough to gauge his options for escape.

"That's more like it." Ezekiel's lip curled up on one corner. "Now you know who's boss."

Cole kept his comments to himself.

Ezekiel stepped back, allowing Cole to walk out in front of him.

As he passed the doctor's cell, Cole glanced sideways.

A pretty woman with long auburn hair stood with her hands on the bars, watching as he walked by. Her brow was creased, concern evident in her eyes. She didn't say a word as he walked past.

Out of the corner of his eye, he saw Ezekiel bring the cattle prod up, aiming for Staci.

Cole flung his arm back, knocking the business end of the prod and taking the full charge in the process.

Staci jumped back, her eyes wide.

Ezekiel's lips pulled back from his teeth in a feral smile. "You shouldn't have done that."

Then he hit Cole again and again with the tip of the cattle prod until Cole fell to his knees, his muscles jerking, the pain immense.

"Stop, you bastard!" Staci screamed. "You'll kill him."

One of the other men approached. "Yeah, man, we need him to work."

Ezekiel finally let up and stood back, his face red with rage. "He needed a lesson."

"We need him able to work. Cyrus won't like it if we have to bury him."

"Cole?" Staci dropped to her knees behind the bars. "Talk to me, soldier."

"I'm okay," he bit out.

"Get up," Ezekiel demanded.

Cole struggled to stand, his muscles still wobbly and tingling. He made it to his feet and staggered after the others as they were herded out of the tunnel into bright daylight.

Cole squinted, blinded by the sun after being in the dark for so long. He struggled to take in his surroundings.

As soon as the last man exited the tunnel, Ezekiel swung a huge metal door over the opening, closing it to the outside. A lock hung open on the hasp.

When Ezekiel went to close the lock, another man with thick brown hair and brown eyes approached. Cole recognized him as the other man who had been talking to Elizabeth in front of the lodge. He also wore a taser gun hooked to his belt. "Leave it," he commanded. "Elizabeth will be here shortly. They have need of the doctor."

Ezekiel let go of the lock and fell in step behind Cole.

The valley men herded the prisoners around the side of the mountain and into a large building. The equipment inside appeared to be the kind used to process ore to extract precious metals.

The men were marched to the back of the building, where it butted up against the mountain. They entered the mountain through the reinforced mineshaft and walked back several yards to an elevator cage.

The prisoners were taken down two at a time, with two valley guys standing guard inside the cage with them. Cole was in the second round with a young man who'd said his name was Sean.

He lifted his chin and acknowledged the younger man. "Sean."

The valley guard corrected him. "John, not Sean. His name is John. And you're now Paul." He stared at Cole.

Cole frowned. "Is that a way of justifying the abduction of people to do your mining for free? By giving them biblical names? Does that somehow make it right?"

Ezekiel tagged him with the cattle prod. "Have some respect, *Paul*. Enough talking."

Cole fought hard to control the urge to slug the man. He had to focus on his task, or he'd quickly get into an altercation with the Glory Valley man and kick his ass.

The elevator took them down to the bottom of the shaft, a couple of hundred feet from where they'd started.

They stepped out of the cage into another tunnel illuminated by electric lighting.

The other men were already at work wielding pickaxes and shovels and filling bins with rock.

After Sean showed him what to do, Cole went to work, pounding rock and loading it for transport up to the processing plant above. The guards kept a close eye on them, ready to zap them with the cattle prods or the taser if they didn't work hard enough or caused any trouble.

Nowhere along the way had Cole noticed anything smaller than the pickax that he could hide in his shirt and take back to the cell to use to break bars or pick locks.

He'd have to attempt an escape while the guards moved them to and from the working mine. In case his efforts to escape failed, and he wanted Jake and his team to find him, he'd have to dig the GPS tracker out of the back of his neck and drop it outside the entrance to the cell tunnel.

Twelve grueling hours later, Cole realized why the others hadn't been able to escape. Working a mine was exhausting work. They didn't have any energy left to fight their way out of the hell where they were imprisoned.

It was dark and getting cold by the time the guards returned them to the cells.

As he passed Staci's cell, he could see the lock hung loose and the gate was ajar. She was gone.

CHAPTER 6

Staci had spent the morning talking with Mark, trying to keep the man's spirits up and failing miserably. He was in pain, and it wasn't getting better. If he didn't get to a hospital soon, he could die.

After noon, Elizabeth arrived with Cyrus. Staci was escorted from her cell and loaded into an old pickup, sitting on a bench seat between Elizabeth and Cyrus.

"Where are we going?" she asked.

"You're needed at the Danvers' place," Cyrus answered.

"I could have handled it without her help," Elizabeth murmured. She sat with her arms crossed over her chest, a frown denting her brow.

"We have a doctor; we might as well use her," Cyrus said, his tone stern.

Elizabeth sat in sullen silence the rest of the ride through town and out into the foothills.

The Danvers had a small, clapboard house nestled in the trees. If there had been paint on the wood siding, it had long since weathered away. A child stood on the porch, wearing tattered clothing, an old jacket that had seen better days and shoes that looked too big for her little feet. When she saw the truck coming, she ran into the house.

A young man stepped out onto the porch, a worried frown pulling his eyebrows together.

Cyrus got out of the truck, crossed to the young man and climbed the steps to the porch.

Elizabeth took a little longer getting out.

Staci slid across the bench and dropped out of the truck.

"We brought your bag." Elizabeth reached into the back of the truck and pulled out Staci's leather satchel.

Staci took the bag and hugged it to her chest. The bag was a connection to her father, and she'd hated thinking she might have lost it for good.

Elizabeth climbed the porch steps and nodded toward the man standing there. "Abe."

"Margaret's in the bedroom," the man said.

"Are the contractions coming closer together?" Elizabeth asked.

"Ask Rebecca. I don't know about these things."

He placed a straw cowboy hat on his head and tipped his chin toward Cyrus. "I have work to do."

Cyrus walked away with the man. "Did you get the tractor running?"

"Nah. Haven't had the chance to replace that hose you brought back on your supply run."

The two men headed for the barn.

If Staci wanted to escape, now was the time to do it while the men weren't watching, and the women were occupied.

A woman cried out inside the house, the sound tugging at Staci's heart.

She was a doctor. Her calling was to help the sick and injured. Or, in this case, it sounded like she needed to help a pregnant woman deliver a baby.

"I can do this myself," Elizabeth muttered. "I've done it many times before."

"I have no doubt you can," Staci said. "But could we see the patient? Between the two of us, we might help."

Elizabeth reluctantly led her into the house and to a room at the back where a woman lay on the bed. Beside her stood a girl in her teens.

"This is my daughter, Rebecca," Elizabeth said. "She can help."

Staci nodded toward the girl. "Nice to meet you, Rebecca." She smiled at the pregnant woman writhing in the bed. "Hi, I'm Dr. Miller. Elizabeth,

Rebecca and I are going to help the best we can. What is your name?"

"Naomi," she said.

As Staci examined the woman, she realized she wasn't much older than Rebecca. "Naomi, is this your first baby?"

"Yes," she cried out as another contraction struck her.

For the next two hours, Staci, Elizabeth and Rebecca worked to help deliver a tiny baby boy.

The young mother collapsed in the bed, too tired to hold her child.

Elizabeth cleaned the baby while Staci delivered the placenta and cleaned the mother. By the time they were finished, it was dark outside.

Staci had been too busy working with the birth that she hadn't had time to look for something she could hide on her person that she could use to pick the lock on her cell or pry a bar loose.

Rebecca appeared in the doorway to the bedroom carrying plates of food. "I fixed a meal for everyone," she said.

They helped Naomi recline in her bed and gave her a plate filled with beans and cornbread.

"I would like to wash up before I eat," Staci said.

Elizabeth tipped her head toward the bathroom. "Go ahead." She looked into Staci's eyes. "And thank you."

Staci could tell how hard it must have been for

Elizabeth to say that. She didn't make a big deal about it but headed for the bathroom, searching for anything she could use to get away and run.

In the bathroom, she washed her hands and arms all the way up to her elbows. After she dried her hands, she searched through the drawers for anything she could use in her determination to escape and get help for the prisoners and, especially, Mark and his son. She hoped she could make it happen before things got worse.

In one drawer, she found a metal nail file and a hairpin. She quickly slipped both inside her shirt under her bra. Then she hurried back to the bedroom before Elizabeth got suspicious and came looking for her.

They shared the meal with the mother, talking her through the care and feeding of her baby boy.

Elizabeth would stay with the young mother through the first night to help her.

Eventually, the two men returned to the house.

Abe went to his wife and baby and smiled down at them.

"It's getting late," Cyrus said. "Time to head back."

Staci gathered her satchel and started to follow Cyrus.

He stared at the bag. "Give the bag to Rebecca."

"I'd like to keep it with me," she said.

"Give it to Rebecca," he insisted.

Staci had no choice but to hand the bag to the teen.

Rebecca took the satchel, meeting Staci's gaze. "Thank you for what you did today."

"Enough. We're wasting time." Cyrus grabbed Staci's arm and half-dragged her out of the house to the truck.

Elizabeth hadn't checked Staci for anything pilfered.

All the way back to the mountain and the tunnel with the cells, Staci worried that the file would fall out and give her away.

Once they arrived, Cyrus walked her into the tunnel with a flashlight, opened the cell and gave her a shove.

Staci staggered into the darkness, clutching a hand to her breast. She didn't breathe until Cyrus had gone, and she was left in the dark with a file and a hairpin and no idea how to pick a lock.

"Hey, Mark," she called out.

"Yeah," he said, his voice weak.

"How's it going?" she asked. "How's the leg?"

"I'm still here," he said. "It still hurts."

Her chest tightened. They had to get him to a hospital soon, or he could lose the leg or his life. The more he sat, the more chance of infection, clotting or, potentially, a pulmonary embolism.

"Cole?"

"Still here."

"Learn anything?" she asked.

"Mining is hard work," he said.

Chuckles and groans sounded down the line of prisoners.

"What about you?"

"Delivered a baby," she said.

"Congratulations," Cole said.

"The mother couldn't have been more than sixteen." She sighed. "Elizabeth's teenage daughter helped. I think she's grooming her to be another midwife."

The heavy metal door squealed as someone opened it.

Staci hid the file and hairpin in her bra and stood away from the gate.

The guards brought the same cardboard boxes, this time containing stew and a bread roll.

Though she'd eaten earlier, she ate the stew and saved the bread roll, thinking she might need it if she could work the lock free and escape.

Once their dinner was completed, the guards cleared the bowls away, closed the metal door, and darkness pressed in around her.

Rather than let the gloom get to her, she took out the file and the hairpin and went to work on the lock. Occasionally, the lock banged against the bars.

"What are you doing?" Cole asked.

"Working on the lock," she said. "I have a nail file and a hairpin. Any suggestions?

"Sorry, I've never picked a lock."

"No?" She laughed and wiggled the file in the padlock, hoping for a miracle.

After half an hour, she took a break, rolled her neck and shoulders and inhaled a long deep breath.

"Any luck?" Mark asked.

"Not yet," she said.

"Don't give up," Sean said from the other side of Mark.

"I won't." She snorted. "After all, I have all night."

"When you get it unlocked, we still have to get out of the tunnel. The metal door is locked from the outside," Cole pointed out.

"Don't be a Debbie Downer," Staci said. "I'll let you figure out that obstacle while I get through this one."

"I wonder if this tunnel connects to other tunnels that could lead out through another exit." Staci recognized Will Mathis's voice from further down the line of cells.

"Without lights, we could fall into a vertical shaft," Robert Bagley said. "At which point, we wouldn't need to worry about getting out. We'd be dead."

"Hey, let's not be negative," Staci said.

"Hard not to be," Mark said. "It's not like we haven't tried to escape. Each of us has tried when they moved us from the tunnel to the mine shaft. If they don't render us immobile with the cattle prods or taser, they beat us to a pulp or waterboard us."

"I'd rather take the beating, cattle prod or taser over waterboarding," Sean said quietly.

"None of the choices are good," Staci said. "We're getting out of here if it's the last thing I do."

"Might be the last thing you do," Robert muttered just loud enough they all could hear.

Silence followed.

Staci went back to work on the lock, determined to trip it and get the hell out. The door would be another worry. They'd tackle it next.

Cole paced his cell. He'd bumped into the wall several times and now had the number of steps before he turned memorized. Though he was exhausted, the thought of Staci picking the lock made him anxious and frustrated. He wished he could have a crack at it if she couldn't get the lock opened.

He could hear her working the lock over the next hour or so, along with several muttered curses. When he heard the clatter of metal against rock, he froze.

"Shoot," Staci muttered.

"What happened?" Cole asked.

"I dropped the file." Several moments later, he heard her sigh. "Found it."

"Jesus, Doc," Robert said. "Take your time. No pressure. Just our lives hanging in the balance."

"Not helping, Bob," Will said.

"Don't call me Bob," Robert said.

Will snorted. "Would you rather I called you Abraham?"

"Shut up, *Elijah*," Robert shot back.

"Look, this could take all night," Staci said. "You guys should sleep. If I don't get this open, you'll need to be rested for work."

"I thought the new guy came to rescue you," Robert said. "Seems like the doc is going to rescue us instead."

Cole's fists clenched.

"I'm sure he would if he had the file," the doctor said. "And we're not out of here yet."

Robert hadn't said anything Cole hadn't already thought, but Staci defending his lack of a plan to rescue them hit him square in his pride.

He reached a hand to the back of his neck and slid his fingernail into his skin, digging for the tiny GPS tracking chip. Once he found it, he slid it into his pocket. If they went back to work the next day, he'd drop the device outside the tunnel. His team would be looking for him at the pickup point that afternoon. When he didn't show, they'd regroup and follow the tracker to the tunnel.

In the meantime, he listened intently for the sound of a lock clicking open.

Another hour passed with the quiet scraping of the metal file in the lock and the soft curses from the doctor. The other men hadn't said a word and had probably taken Staci's advice and were sleeping in preparation for another workday in the mine.

If he were smart, he'd be doing the same.

"Damn it," Staci muttered.

"We need to teach you some new curse words," he said softly.

"Right? I keep using the same ones, and it's not helping." She sighed. "I don't get it. They make this look easy in the movies. How do thieves get through these so quickly?"

Cole smiled at the image he had of the pretty redhead struggling with the lock in the dark. "They use bolt cutters. I'm sure it helps to have light to work with, too."

"Actually, the dark is making me more aware of sound and touch. Sometimes, I can almost feel the lock catching on the file or hear a click like it's almost engaging. If I could see, I might not be as aware."

"They say thieves who can crack a safe do it by touch and sound."

"Cracking a safe might be easier," Staci said.

"Take a break. Rest your hands. Then go back at it fresh," he suggested.

"I'm running out of time. If I don't get it open soon, I won't have time to work the locks on the other cells."

"I'd help if I could," he said. "I'm impressed you were able to find something to use for picking a lock.

I looked on the way to and from the mine and didn't find anything smaller than a pickax. I couldn't fit a pickax into my jacket or pants, or I would have."

Her chuckle warmed the darkness. "I could picture you trying. How would you do that?"

His lips twitched. "I thought maybe I'd hide it beneath the back of my jacket with the axe end at my shoulders, sleeve-to-sleeve, and the handle down the back of my pants."

"Why didn't you do it?" Staci laughed. "I'm sure the valley guys wouldn't have noticed at all."

"If we don't get out of this tonight, I'll give it a try tomorrow."

"I'll hold you to it," she said. "If we're able to escape, I'm worried about the others. Mostly about Mark."

"If we can get away into the night, we'd take him with us."

"I don't think he'd make it. And we couldn't carry him all the way. We wouldn't get far."

"Then we'd have to come back for him."

"That's also what I'm worried about. If all of us get away but Mark, they might want to get rid of him." Her voice faded. "And then there's his son..."

"Staci, we have a little bit of a backup plan."

"A backup plan?" She snorted softly. "We don't even have an escape plan."

"When I was dropped off on the road into the valley, Thorn, my teammate, promised to come back for me in a couple of days. If I wasn't at the drop-off point or he hadn't heard from me, he'd come looking for me."

"Then we'll be all right. They'll find us."

"I'm not so sure," Cole said. "What if they're caught in the same trap as I was?"

"They wouldn't come alone, would they?"

"I don't think so. But the people of Glory Valley are very good at hiding their victims, and no one talks."

"And if someone comes poking around," Staci said slowly, "they might do something more drastic."

"We are in a mine tunnel. An explosion could cause a cave-in…"

"And we'd die in here." The sound of metal scraping metal started up again. "And I thought Robert was depressing."

"Look, the first day was my chance to look for opportunities. At the very least, we might just have to fight our way out."

"Not everyone is trained to do that."

"I know. They usually only have one guard for each of us. If we turn on them, we could potentially overpower them."

"They don't come for me until they need my services."

"We'd get the keys and get you out." He sure as hell wouldn't leave her there with the crazies. They knew the mountains and the mine. There was no telling where they'd hide her. "We only have to get away far enough and long enough for my team to get here and find us. Then we'll bring in the state police, FBI and anyone else who gives a damn to get Mark and his son out of here."

"And if we try and fail...I don't know about you, but I think Cyrus and Ezekiel wouldn't be happy."

"That's why we can't just try." Cole's hands fisted. "We have to make it happen."

A loud click sounded in the darkness.

"Cole?" Staci called out, her voice shaking.

"What's wrong?" He leaned against the bars of his cell, wishing he could see in the black abyss.

"The lock," she whispered. "It's open."

CHAPTER 7

Staci's heart raced as she slid the padlock off the hasp and pushed the gate open. She eased out of the cell.

"It's strange," she said. "I'm a little frightened outside my cell. Is that weird?"

"Not at all. When you can't see, you can get disoriented really fast."

"And a little dizzy," she admitted.

"Keep a hand on the bars or the wall. You don't want to get disoriented or lost in the dark," Cole warned. "Follow my voice."

With her hand on the bars, until they ended, and the concrete wall began, she worked her way toward Cole's voice. He kept talking softly, the warmth of his tone easing her heart rate, making her feel a little safer.

When she reached his cell, his hands found hers,

and he squeezed them gently. His fingers were strong and warm.

For a moment, she held onto him, absorbing his strength. Tears welled in her eyes. She didn't try to hold them back. No one would see them.

"Are you okay?" he asked.

She swallowed hard on the lump clogging her throat and squared her shoulders. "I am. Let's get your lock open."

"Do you want me to do it?" he asked.

"No. Let me. It's like I said, the more I worked on it, the better I could feel what was going on inside."

She had to let go of his hands to move to the other end of the iron gate where the padlock hung.

As she worked on the lock, Cole's hand reached out to touch her arm.

At first, her hands shook, and she feared she'd forget how the mechanism felt against the file. After trying for another hour or more, she finally handed him the file. "I can't do this. You try. If mine is the only lock we open tonight, it does us no good."

He took the file from her hand. "We still have time."

"Not much. It must be getting close to morning. Ezekiel and his buddies will be back soon to feed us and take you guys to the mine."

"We'll get this lock open," he said.

As he worked, Staci reached through the bars to touch his arm as he had done hers. She liked how thick his muscles were and how he made her feel safe, even when he was locked behind the bars.

After he'd tried for another thirty to forty-five minutes, she closed her hands around his. "Let me."

He gave her the file and ran his hand up her arm to her shoulder. "You're an amazing woman, Dr. Miller."

She laughed. "I don't feel amazing."

"You are. You came to the mountains to help people."

"Who have now abducted and imprisoned me," she reminded him.

"But you're still helping them. You delivered a baby yesterday."

"I have to help. It's what I do."

"It's who you are," he said.

His words warmed her heart. Her ex-fiancé hadn't understood that about her even after dating for two years. Yet, here was this stranger who *got* her in such a short time. "You're a trained soldier. How did they capture you?"

"I more or less let them." He sighed. "It was the quickest way I could think of to find you."

"They could've killed you rather than brought you here." She shook her head, sick at the idea he'd put himself at risk for her. "You were taking a huge chance."

"I'm not like Mark," he said. "I don't have as much to lose. It makes it easier to take chances."

Her fingers paused in their work. "Cole, your life is worth something."

"I don't have anyone who depends on me. If I die, others won't be impacted."

"*I'll* be impacted," she said. Her hand closed around his.

He chuckled. "You just met me."

"Yeah, but I like you. Talking to you has been the only thing that has kept me from freaking out. I don't think I've ever talked to anyone like I've talked with you. I always feel awkward when I talk to men."

"Why? You're beautiful, intelligent and amazing."

"And introverted and tongue-tied with men."

"You were engaged."

"I think he only liked that I was a doctor. When I said I wanted to help the underserved, he dropped me like a hot potato. He wanted me to work in Denver, making a lot more money."

"He didn't deserve you," Cole said. "You were lucky he ditched you."

"I know. It wouldn't have lasted. We wanted different things. We weren't compatible." She went back to work, fully aware of the time ticking by and getting more nervous as it passed. "What about you? You're still young, and you're a good-looking guy. Why don't you let yourself fall in love again?"

He didn't answer for a long time.

Her fingers faltered. Had she stepped over the line? It wasn't her business to know why he wasn't dating, even if she really wanted to know. "I'm sorry. That was too personal."

"No. It's okay," he said. "I lost my world when Lisa and Tyler died."

"You must have loved her so very much."

"I did. She was strong enough to live on her own when I was deployed. Even with a child, she didn't let anything get her down. And when I came home, she was there to welcome me, and we stepped back into our relationship like I'd never been gone. I was so lucky to have found her. So many of my married teammates either divorced during their first married deployment or found it hard to assimilate into the marriage and family when they returned. I had it good."

Staci's heart hurt for Cole. At the same time, she envied Lisa. She'd had the whole-hearted love of this man. "Would Lisa have wanted you to grieve for her for the rest of your life? Or would she have wanted you to move on? Surely, she wouldn't have expected you to grieve for her and your son to your dying day. She would've wanted you to love and be loved, to be happy." As soon as the words were out of her mouth, Staci wished she could take them back.

Cole had loved his wife and son so much that he hadn't been able to get on with life.

"Up until recently, I remained a member of Delta Force. I wasn't home often enough to have a life to *move on.* Yes, Lisa would've wanted me to be happy. She believed in love and happiness.

"I should've believed in it as much as she had. I should've given up on Delta Force a lot earlier. If I had, she wouldn't have been alone, driving herself and my son in those terrible conditions. I should've been there."

Staci felt the pain in his voice. The self-blame because he had not been there for his family.

"You had a job to do, a mission to accomplish and a country to represent," Staci said softly. "As you said, Lisa understood."

"I had a family," Cole said. "Now, they're gone."

"You could've been home when it happened. You can't blame yourself. Your wife wouldn't have blamed you. And you can't blame yourself for your friend's death in battle." She stopped working the lock to listen to Cole's response.

"None of them should've died."

"But they did, and you lived. And you can't move on because you feel you should've died, too."

"In effect, I did."

"Only because you let yourself." Staci's heart hurt for Cole, but he had to understand. "You are still here. Alive. Capable of so much more in life. You're still here for a reason. I'm selfish enough to want to believe that reason is to save me." She maneuvered the file once more, and the lock mechanism clicked.

Staci's hands froze. "Did you hear that?" she whispered.

"I heard it," he said. "Is it the lock?"

She nodded, then realized he couldn't hear her shake her head. "It opened."

His hands reached for the padlock, closing around her hands holding it in her palms. He pulled her hands up to the bars. "Dr. Staci Miller, you are worth so much more than money. You are strong, invincible and one hundred percent kind. Your fiancé was a fool, not you." He brought her hand up to his lips and kissed her knuckles. "Thank you for believing in a stranger."

Her heart melted. She hadn't known what she'd wanted to do with her life. Trevor's rejection had shaken her confidence in her decision. Cole's words helped reinforce her determination and her belief that she was doing the right thing. "Thank you."

He chuckled. "No. Thank *you*." He cupped her cheek. "Why are we standing here with the bars between us when we don't have to?"

"Here." Cole handed her the file and slipped the lock off the hasp, opened the gate, flipped the latch back and hung the padlock on the hasp. At first glance, the lock appeared to be in place and secure.

The sound of metal clanking against metal made Staci tremble and her pulse race.

"Hold onto the file, get back to your cell and hang your padlock like this. Hurry."

"What about the others?" she asked.

"No time to work their locks," he said. "Go."

Clutching the file in her hand, Staci raced back to her cell and quickly arranged her lock and latch as Cole had done, positioning it as the huge metal door swung open and light from headlamps flashed into the tunnel.

Staci stood back from her gate, her mind racing. They hadn't had time to go over a plan. She didn't know what Cole had in mind.

Inhaling a deep breath, she held it and waited for Cole's next move. She'd be ready. For what? She wasn't sure. But this was their chance. They had to take it while they could. Once the valley men discovered the locks had been compromised, they wouldn't let it happen again.

And there would be consequences for their actions. Staci shivered.

Then she squared her shoulders and prepared to fight.

COLE HUNG BACK from his gate and waited for the guard to come to him.

The same as the day before, one guard banged metal on metal, the sound deafening as it reverberated off the tunnel's rock walls.

He covered his ears until the noise stopped and

footsteps sounded as the guards brought the cardboard trays to each cell.

He prayed the guard serving Staci's cell wouldn't notice that the lock wasn't like they'd left it the night before. The last guard bringing his food tray had to reach Cole before the fun could begin.

He held his breath and waited.

"Get up!" Ezekiel yelled. "You have three minutes to eat. Move it!" he carried a tray in one hand, a cattle prod in the other, banging the cattle prod against the metal gates as he moved past each cell.

When he came to Staci's, he paused. "You, too. Elizabeth will be here soon. She has plans for you today."

Cole counted the seconds, praying Ezekiel didn't linger at Staci's gate.

"Did she say what those plans were? Is someone sick?" she asked.

"Ask Elizabeth. I don't keep up with the medical needs of Glory Valley. That's her job and now yours. Just be ready."

"I'll be ready," Staci said.

Ezekiel's footsteps sounded, on the move again, toward the last occupied cell. Cole's.

Cole stood by the gate, his muscles bunched, his hands at his sides.

Ezekiel stopped in front of his gate, a sneer lifting one corner of his mouth. "You gonna be mouthy again today?"

"Depends on you," Cole said.

"Good. Makes my day to use you as an example for the others."

Cole smiled, blinded by the light shining in his face from Ezekiel's headlamp. "I live to make your day shine."

Ezekiel frowned. "Yeah, well, don't get too smug. There's lots of work to get through today. Can't have you wasting energy running off at the mouth."

"I'm ready to get this day started."

Ezekiel's eyes narrowed as he bent to place the cardboard tray on the floor at his feet.

Cole leaped forward, grabbed the gate and shoved it open hard and fast. The gate slammed into Ezekiel, knocking him off his feet.

Cole was out of the cell and onto Ezekiel as he rose from the ground.

Before the valley man could regain his balance, Cole clasped his wrist and yanked his arm up and behind his back. With his other hand, he snatched the taser from where it was hooked on Ezekiel's belt.

The other men yelled.

"What the hell?" the one who'd bent to slide Staci's tray under her gate started to rise, his hand grasping the taser clipped to his belt.

Before he could straighten, Staci slammed her gate into him.

The man staggered backward, his taser flying

from his grip, landing at Staci's feet. She grabbed the gun and the man's cattle prod.

When he moved, she hit him with the prod.

"Stay back," Cole said as he pushed Ezekiel in front of him, holding his arm jacked up behind his back. He applied enough pressure to make the man stand on his toes to ease the pain.

Moving quickly, he rushed toward the other three guards.

The one in front of Staci crab-walked backward as fast as he could go, running into the next guard and making him lose his balance. He kicked the man on the ground and struggled to right himself.

"Shoot him," Ezekiel screeched.

The guard regained his balance and fired his taser.

The prongs hit Ezekiel square in the chest.

The man dropped to the ground, rendered immobile.

The man who'd fired his taser at Ezekiel threw his taser to the ground and brought up his cattle prod.

Cole charged the three men. He kicked the man rising from the ground in the jaw.

He fell back and lay still.

The guy who'd fired the taser came at Cole.

Cole ducked beneath the cattle prod, grabbed the man's wrist and yanked him past him, slamming him headfirst into the rock wall of the tunnel. His cattle prod fell from his grip and skittered across the tunnel floor.

When he tried to rise, Staci hit him with Ezekiel's prod and kept the pressure on him until he collapsed to the ground.

Cole didn't have time to deal with the one behind him when the fourth guard rushed toward him, cattle prod at the ready.

Ducking, Cole swept his arm up, slamming the long metal stick upward and knocking it from the man's hands.

The valley guy turned on Cole and grabbed him around the neck. While the man had him in a choke-hold, Cole ran backward, ramming him into the rock wall again and again.

Though the man's hold around his neck was weakening, so too was Cole's blood oxygen level.

Then he felt the man lean backward, pulling hard on his neck. Suddenly, his arms loosened enough that Cole broke free.

Staci had the man by the hair, hitting him with the business end of the cattle prod.

"Get back, Staci!" Cole yelled.

She jumped back, releasing her hold on the man's hair.

Cole hunkered low, plowed into the man, and shoved him into Staci's empty cell, slamming him against the wall.

He slid to the ground, unconscious.

When he turned, he found Staci pulling on Ezekiel's legs, trying to drag him into the cell. Already, his body twitched. It wouldn't be long before he was mobile again. The other guards were starting to revive as well.

"Forget it." Cole emerged from the cell. "We have to go."

Staci gathered another cattle prod and hurried after Cole. "What about the others?"

"Yeah, what about us?" Robert asked.

"No time." Cole grabbed Staci's arm. "We'll come back with help."

Cole ran toward the tunnel opening then slowed long enough to check for other valley men. With no others in the immediate vicinity, Cole left the tunnel with Staci at his side. He dug in his pocket for the tiny tracking device and dropped it outside the tunnel door.

"Can you run?" he asked, taking off at a trot.

"When my life depends on it, yes."

The tunnel entrance was out of sight of the town below the mountain. The hillsides were barren around the mining tunnel. They had to get to the next plateau and drop down into another depression or ravine to move out of sight.

Cole could feel the effects of the altitude on his lungs. The mine and the tunnel where they'd been held captive were a couple of thousand feet higher than the valley below. Running became more of a challenge at twelve thousand feet.

The men who'd worked the mines all their lives had an advantage. Their lungs were used to the higher altitude.

As soon as they got far enough away from the mine entrances, they'd have to descend or risk altitude sickness. Cole had noticed rifles on racks in some of the trucks the men drove. With no trees or clumps of boulders nearby, they would be easy to pick off for someone skilled at shooting.

Staci kept up with him, though he could tell the altitude was making it hard for her to breathe.

Shouts below alerted him that the guards had recovered enough to come after them. Their trucks would not make the climb on the steep hills. Hopefully, they didn't have ATVs that would have no problem following them.

Just a little further, and they'd top the rise.

Cole prayed there was a ravine on the other side that would lead down the opposite side of the mountain the mine was located in. He knew there were other peaks even higher beyond the mountain they were climbing, and those were further away.

Small engines revved below as Cole reached the ridgeline and pulled Staci up beside him.

He glanced back and swore when he spotted two ATVs starting up the hillside.

He and Staci had a lead on them, but they wouldn't for long.

On the other side of the ridge, the land dropped down at a steep, grass-covered slope into a ravine. The ravine disappeared into a rocky crevasse below the tree line, with pine trees growing on either side.

Cole pointed. "We have to make it there before they catch up to us."

She drew in a deep breath.

The echo of a shot fired bounced off the mountainside as a rock kicked up at Staci's heels.

She jumped and launched herself forward down the hillside.

The grass was green, spongy and slick with morning dew.

Staci's feet slipped out from under her. She sat down hard and slid down the hill.

Cole ran after her but couldn't match her downhill speed. Finally, he sat and slid down the slope, his ass taking a beating on every rocky bump. His heavier weight gave gravity an extra oomph, and he could almost close the distance between him and Staci.

The slope leveled slightly near the bottom just before the grass ended and the ravine dropped into the rocky crevasse.

Staci rolled onto her stomach and dug her fingers into the ground to bring herself to a complete stop.

Cole did the same.

As soon as he had slowed enough, he leaped to his feet and helped Staci up. Together they ran for the trees.

The ATVs had reached the top of the ridge and were headed down the steep slope.

They had only seconds to lose themselves in the trees and the craggy sides of the ravine. The ATVs wouldn't be able to follow them there. The two men would have to continue on foot. It would give them more of a chance.

As they reached the trees, Cole risked a glance over his shoulder.

The ATVs were nearing the bottom of the slope.

They were close enough that Cole could make out Ezekiel on one and Cyrus on the other. They had gun boots mounted on the sides of each four-wheeler.

"It's Cyrus and Ezekiel," Staci said. "They look mad."

"Yeah, and they're not carrying tasers." Cole grabbed Staci's hand and ran through the trees, hoping they could put as much distance as possible between them and the valley men before they ran out of breath.

CHAPTER 8

STACI'S LUNGS BURNED. She wished she'd been on a better workout routine before coming to the mountains. She'd never thought she'd be running for her life above ten thousand feet.

The trees were great for cover and concealment but not so good for knowing where they were going. At least the ravine had them moving in one direction, not going around in circles.

Another thought pushed itself into her oxygen-deprived mind. Would the ravine lead to the floor of the valley? If so, would other valley men be waiting with their guns to shoot them as they emerged?

Staci tried not to think about that and focus instead on getting enough air into her lungs to keep up with Cole. She didn't want to be the reason they were caught.

It wasn't just her lungs burning. Her calves and

thighs were on fire from all the running, climbing and navigating the steep sides of the ravine.

The more exhausted she became, the more she slipped and fell. Staci didn't want to slow down or take a break. Her body could make that determination for her. She wasn't sure how much longer she would last before she collapsed.

They came to a point where they had to cross another ravine that fed into the main one they had been following.

Cole leaped across the three-foot-wide expanse.

Staci stopped and stared at the gap, and then sighed and stepped down into the rocks rather than leaping across. Just as Cole reached down to grab her hand, she stepped on a loose stone, and it gave way and started the other rocks beneath it sliding down the ravine.

Staci pitched sideways and would have fallen except for the hand that grabbed hers and pulled her across and into Cole's arms.

He crushed her to his chest and held her for a moment. Her heart raced pressed against his. "Thank you," she said. She tipped her head backward and looked up into his deep brown eyes. "I'm sorry I'm slowing down."

"It's okay. We're going to make it. You're doing great." He smiled down at her and pushed a strand of her hair back from her face, tucking it behind her ear. Then he bent and brushed his lips across her forehead. He leaned back and smiled down at her. "Hang in there." Then he touched his lips to hers.

The electricity that sparked between them must have shocked him as much as it did her. He straightened, his eye flaring.

Her fingers curled into his shirt. Her racing heart now had nothing to do with running through the mountains. It had to do with a surge of desire burning through her veins. What was wrong with her? She should be running, hiding, moving. Instead, she stood still, staring up into this stranger's eyes, willing him to kiss her again.

And he did.

This time he didn't just brush his mouth across hers, he crushed her lips in a kiss that demanded a response from her.

She slid her hands up his chest and around his neck, bringing him closer, opening to him.

His tongue swept in to take hers in a sensual caress that made her tingle from her head all the way down to her toes.

When he raised his head, she inhaled, remembering how to breathe. "What was that?" she said, her voice breathy, her pulse pounding.

"I don't know," he said, shoving a hand through his hair. "I'd do it again, but I think I hear our tail crashing through the woods."

He took her hand, and they ran, leaping logs, climbing over boulders and dodging through trees.

When they came to a ten-foot drop-off, Cole jumped and landed on a soft bed of leaves and moss. He turned and held up his arms. "Sit and slide off. I'll catch you."

Staci did so and landed in his arms. He lowered her to the ground and looked at the side of the hill.

Shouts sounded nearby.

Too close.

Staci started to run and was brought up short by Cole's hand on her arm. He pressed a finger to his lips and pointed at the hill they'd just dropped down from.

A tree clung to the ledge above; its roots had grown over the ledge and found their way to the bottom of the ten-foot drop-off creating a curtain of roots and moss, concealing a cave-like hollow large enough to fit two people.

Cole parted the curtain of roots and moss and motioned for her to get in.

The thought of all the creepy bugs and snakes that could be hiding in there made Staci hesitate.

More shouts above made her dive into the recess and scoot over as far as she could to allow Cole to fold his long body in beside hers. He let the curtain of roots and moss close over their hiding place and pushed decaying leaves and dirt up in front of them.

Then he pulled Staci into his arms and held her close. The dampness of the roots and dirt sank through her clothes, making her shiver.

Cole's arms around her warmed her. She snuggled close and strained to hear Cyrus and Ezekiel crashing through the woods, moving closer to them.

"I saw them a minute ago," Ezekiel said. They can't be far."

Staci's breath caught. They were standing so close they had to be on the ledge above where she and Cole hid.

"Keep moving," Cyrus's gruff voice said. "We'll catch up soon. They can't leave the valley."

Footsteps crunched over twigs and gravel as the two men found their way down from the ledge without jumping as Cole and Staci had done.

Then they appeared in front of the hollow, moving away, carrying rifles.

They lay for a long time in the recess behind the curtain of roots until they couldn't hear Cyrus and Ezekiel's footsteps or voices.

"What now?" Staci whispered.

"We stay put until dusk. Then we make our move."

"It gets cold at night," she reminded him. In the tunnel cell, they'd had a wool blanket to keep them warm.

"If we're going to make it out of the valley to somewhere we can find a phone and call for help, we'll have to keep moving."

"There weren't any homes along the road leading into the valley," she reminded him.

"The pass is nothing but sheer rock bluffs," Cole noted. "They'll be watching for us to go through there. Traveling by road would make it too easy for them to find us."

"How else will we get out of the valley?" she asked.

He shook his head. "The mountains surrounding the valley reach altitudes between twelve and thirteen thousand feet and are rugged. It would take too long to go over them." He nodded toward the gaps in the trees where they could see patches of sky, blanketed in thick clouds, that seemed to have been descending on them as the morning had progressed into afternoon. "The weather isn't looking great."

"Dusk is fleeting in the valley. Once the sun dips below the peaks, it gets dark fast. Should we get started?"

Cole's arms around her tightened once more and then released her. He parted the roots and moss and crawled out of their hiding place, reaching back to help her out and onto her feet.

"At the very least, we're rested," she said, brushing leaves and dirt from her hands. Her clothes were damp from lying in the dirt. Without Cole's arms around her, a chill seemed to be seeping into her bones. She shivered. "Where to?"

Cole glanced up at the sky. "We need to find a place to hole up. It's getting colder out here, and it looks like rain."

"Shouldn't we just stay here?" She pointed to the hollow.

He shook his head. "It was a great place to hide, but it won't keep us dry. It's damp like the rain soaks through it."

Staci nodded, rubbing her arms to keep warm. "Then we'd better find someplace we can stay warm and dry, or we'll die of hypothermia."

As they left the hollow behind, a gentle rain began to fall.

Staci began to wonder if they should have stayed in the tunnel cells. Though they'd been prisoners, they'd been dry and somewhat warm.

COLE SECOND-GUESSED himself as they moved through the forest, descending even closer to the valley floor. Had he gotten the two of them out of their prison only for them to die of exposure? Walking out of the valley that night was quickly becoming an impossibility as the mist continued, the temperature dropped and the moisture in the air turned to snow.

The best thing he could do now was find shelter where they could get warm and dry. Staci was already pale and turning a little blue. If he didn't get her somewhere they could dry off, she would be in trouble. It had to be before all the light left the sky. With the cloud cover, they would be in complete darkness, as if they were back in the tunnel, only this time, they could easily get lost.

Light was quickly fading when they came to the edge of the forest.

Goats grazed in the lush green, alpine field with no fences holding them in.

Cole remembered Mark's son herding goats across a similar field on the other side of the valley. He wondered if this herd was the same one.

From their vantage point, they could see the town lower down in the valley and the outlying homes scattered higher up the sides of the mountains.

What looked like an abandoned shack made of weathered wood and a tin roof stood near a clump of aspens on the far side of the field. A line of trees snaked along the edge of the field, following a creek. If they stayed with the creek, they could get closer to the shack and make sure it wasn't occupied.

Cole led the way, creeping among the shadows of the evergreens. When they were within twenty yards of the shack, Cole hunkered low and studied the shack.

Beside him, Staci shivered violently.

He had to do something soon. He started to rise when the door to the shack opened.

Ducking low, he waited to see who would emerge.

A tall, thin young man with a mop of dark hair emerged, turned and spoke to someone inside. He leaned in as a female leaned out. They embraced and kissed.

Staci gasped. "That's Dalton, Mark's son," she whispered.

The girl emerged, pulling on a coat as she did.

"And that's Rebecca, Cyrus's daughter." Staci shook her head. "If they get caught...Cyrus and Elizabeth would not be happy."

Dalton hurried across the field to the goats and herded them back toward town in the fading light.

Rebecca pulled the door closed and crossed the field in the opposite direction, heading toward Staci and Cole.

Cole pushed the low branch of a spruce tree aside.

Staci slipped between the branches, and Cole moved in beside her, letting the branch fall back in place.

Rebecca stopped and stared in their direction for a long moment.

Cole and Staci remained perfectly still.

After a few long, agonizing seconds, Rebecca turned slightly, walked to the trees, and ducked into the shadows. She reemerged, leading a horse by its reins.

The young woman swung up in the saddle and sat there as if undecided which direction to go.

Then she reined the horse around and trotted directly for the tree where Cole and Staci hid.

She reined the animal to a stop within a few feet of them and looked out over the field.

"My father and his men are still looking for you, but they're staking out the road leading out of the valley. They've told everyone in the valley that the stranger who arrived yesterday has kidnapped the doctor. You're considered dangerous. They're to shoot first or risk being killed."

Staci moved slightly.

Cole laid a hand on her arm.

Rebecca continued. "The cabin is warm and dry. If you wait until dark, you can light a fire in the fireplace. But not before. If the clouds clear, douse the fire or the smoke will be visible in the starlight. It's dark in the cabin, but if you reach to the right beside the door, there's a miner's headlamp hanging on a hook."

When neither Cole nor Staci spoke, Rebecca said, "I know you're hiding in the tree."

Staci spoke, "You won't tell your father where we are?"

"No," she said. "You probably saw Dalton leaving. If I told my father about you, you could tell him about Dalton and me. My father would probably kill Dalton rather than have his daughter run away with him."

"Are you going to run away with Dalton?" Staci asked softly.

"I would, but he won't leave without his father.

131

And just so you know, not everyone believes what my father is doing is right. They're afraid of him. He and Ezekiel keep us locked down and isolated from the rest of the world. They say it's to protect us." She shook her head. "How is it protecting us when they force us to marry at sixteen to people of their choosing."

"Are they forcing you to marry, Rebecca?" Cole asked.

Rebecca looked away. "My parents told me I will marry Nehemiah, Ezekiel's son, when I turn sixteen next month." Her tone was harsh, and her fingers curled into fists around the reins.

Cole's heart ached for the girl.

"How do you feel about that?" Staci asked.

"If Dalton won't come with me, I'll leave the valley alone." She sat taller in the saddle. "I won't marry Nehemiah or anyone else in this valley. I'm done with Glory Valley. I want out."

"When we get out, we'll come back with help to free Dalton, Mark and the others. What your parents are doing isn't legal. They can't force you to marry anyone. And they shouldn't be forcing children to marry. You're still considered a child, Rebecca. The state protects children."

Rebecca snorted. "The state has done nothing to protect us. They don't even know we exist. And I've heard how they protect children by leaving them with abusive parents who eventually kill them. If I wait for the state to help me, they'll leave me with my parents. Running away is the only way out for me.

"Anyway, I have to get back home. My folks think I'm checking on Naomi and the baby. I did, over an hour ago. I have to get back before they start to search for me. I hope you make it out. And I hope you come back and help Dalton and the others leave this hell my people call home. And if they arrest my father and Ezekiel, good. Maybe then we can have more choices over what we want out of life."

"What about your mother?"

Rebecca's eyes narrowed. "I think without my father, she'd be a better person. Hopefully, time will tell. Good luck." She turned her horse and rode across the pasture.

Cole waited for a few more minutes to ensure no one else was in the area.

By then, Staci was shaking so hard that her teeth rattled. Night had crept in, reducing the shack to a black shadow in the nearly total darkness.

Cole took Staci's hand, shocked at how cold it was. He wrapped his arm around her and hurried her across the twenty yards to the shack, entered through the only door and closed it behind them. Like in the tunnel, they could see nothing.

Cole felt the wall to the right, found the miner's headlamp and switched it on.

Though the inside of the shack wasn't exactly warm, the walls blocked the cold breeze. The fireplace had a fresh stack of wood and kindling ready for someone to light it. In the corner of the one-room shack was a wooden bed frame with a thin mattress folded over. In another corner stood a makeshift table consisting of three four-foot-long planks laid over two stacks of concrete blocks. Two folding camp stools served as chairs. A handwoven blanket hung on a nail on the wall. Cole grabbed the blanket and wrapped it around Staci.

She shivered so violently Cole thought she might fall over from the force of it. While Cole looked around for matches, Staci stood in the middle of the wooden floor.

A shelf on one wall contained a line of books. Another shelf held stacks of canned goods in Mason jars.

"She must have b-been c-coming here for a w-while," Staci said.

Cole finally located a tin can full of matches and another full of dried moss. With a handful of the moss and a match, he bent and lit a match, held it to the moss until it caught and then slid it into the kindling. Soon the kindling caught fire and the logs began to burn.

Staci moved closer.

Cole stood behind her and rubbed her arms through the blanket, and then leaned her into him.

Once the fire was burning, the tiny shack warmed quickly. Staci's shivers slowed until, finally, she relaxed her shoulders and sighed. "I thought I'd never be warm again."

"I'm sorry. I should've found shelter sooner." He shrugged out of his damp jacket and hung it on a peg near the fire.

Staci laid the blanket on the table, slipped out of her jacket and hung it on another peg on the opposite side of the fire. She shivered again.

"If you're like me, you're not going to get warm enough until your clothes are dry."

"I know. They'll dry faster off our bodies than on them." She gave him a crooked grin. "It might be a little soon in our relationship to feel comfortable getting naked in front of you."

"You can use the blanket. I'll turn my back." Cole handed her the blanket. "I'll heat up something for us to eat."

With his back to her, he took one of the jars of black-eyed peas down, found a cast iron pot with a handle and poured the peas in. The fireplace had a metal hook that could be pushed into position over the fire. He hung the handle on the hook and swung it over the fire. Soon, the scent of food cooking filled the tiny space.

"Okay, I'm struggling here," Staci said. "Will you do the honors?"

He turned to find her holding the blanket over her breasts with one hand with her damp clothes draped over her other hand. He took her clothes and hung them close to the fire.

"What about you?" she asked. "There's only one blanket."

"Your clothes will dry quickly. Then we can switch."

She nodded and dragged the blanket up an inch over the swells of her breasts. Her skin was a pale white in the dim light provided by the fire. When he leaned close enough, he could see the dusting of freckles across her shoulders and chest. They intrigued him, making him wonder what each tasted like.

Dragging his gaze away from her shoulders, he used a stick to swing the pot out of the flames. "I believe the peas are warm enough to eat."

"Good. I'm starving."

"We haven't eaten since about this time last night." He found a couple of tin cups. With a ladle he found hanging on a hook on the wall, he scooped peas out of the pot and into the cups and set them on the table. He found another jar filled with pears and put it on the table. "Dessert."

"I feel bad eating Rebecca's food. She obviously uses this shack to get away." Staci waved at the books on the shelf. "Her own private reading nook."

"And her secret space for teenage canoodling," Cole said.

Staci laughed. "Canoodling? Who uses that word?"

His cheeks heated. "My mother used to call it that when I was a teen heading out on dates."

"Is your mother still alive?"

He nodded. "She is. Both my parents are. Since they retired, they've been living in an RV and travel all over the country."

Staci held the blanket with one hand and scooped peas onto her fork with the other. "Siblings?" she asked, then popped the fork full of peas into her mouth.

"One brother who is an aerospace engineer working with one of the commercial space programs. He's the brain; I'm the brawn."

Staci's eyebrows formed a V. "I thought you didn't have anyone who cared about you. Do you have good relationships with your parents and brother?"

He shrugged. "I haven't been good at keeping in touch since Lisa and Tyler died."

"And how long has that been?"

"Three years."

"Tell me it hasn't been three years since you've talked to your family."

He chuckled, though it was a little forced. "I talk to them on their birthdays and Christmas. I just don't have much to say. Most of my work is Top Secret. I can't talk about it with them."

"And you were too busy volunteering for every mission you could get to avoid having a life outside deployments." She cocked her eyebrows. "Am I right?"

He gave her a tight smile. "Yeah. I didn't have much to talk about, so I didn't call."

Staci stared down at the peas in her cup and set her fork down. "Do you know what I'd give to have one more conversation with my mother?" She gave him a watery smile. "I wouldn't even care what we talked about as long as I could hear her voice. You lost part of your family. Don't lose the rest."

Cole reached across the table and covered her hand. "Okay. I'll call as soon as we're out of Insane Valley and back to reality. Just don't cry. I can handle being shot at, shocked with a taser and cattle prod and sliding down a steep hill on my backside—which I'm sure you're as bruised as I am—but I can't handle tears." He lifted her hand and pressed his lips to the backs of her knuckles. "They gut me."

She laughed as a single tear slipped from the corner of her eye. "Sorry."

He reached up and brushed the tear away with his thumb and then released her hand. "Now, finish your peas so we can open up this jar of pears. I haven't had canned pears since my grandmother used to can the ones from the pear tree in her backyard. She said if I picked them, she'd can them. I picked so many pears that we had canned pears for dessert every week for a year."

"Your grandmother sounds wonderful."

His smile softened. "She was. I miss her. And now that you bring it all up, I miss my mother and father, and even my brainiac brother." Cole finished off his peas and opened the jar of pears. "Is it just you and your father?"

She nodded. "Yes. And I bet he's beside himself with worry if he sent you out to find me."

"He was just being precautionary, thinking you might have gotten busy." Cole's mouth twisted.

Staci snorted softly. "By now, he'll be in a full-blown panic." Her brow furrowed. "I hate that he's worried. But I'm glad he sent you."

"Not that I've gotten you out of here yet, but I will." He poured a couple of canned pears into her empty cup. "Better than a fancy restaurant," he said.

Staci smiled. "Absolutely."

Her smile touched him. Between Staci, the pears, peas and a wood-burning fire, he felt like he'd come home. He had to remind himself they weren't safe. They'd have to figure a way out of the valley and soon. Mark's leg wasn't getting better, and he couldn't trust Cyrus and Ezekiel to keep the prisoners alive.

When they'd finished the food, Cole stacked the dirty dishes to the side. He didn't like leaving them dirty, but to clean them, he'd have to take them out to the creek wearing a headlamp. He couldn't risk being spotted even from a distance. They needed rest and time for their clothing to dry before they set out again.

In the meantime, he had a beautiful, semi-naked woman in the same room as he was, and he had to remember he was a gentleman, and they were still strangers. He had to get through the night without him taking advantage of her. But if she were to take advantage of him...

CHAPTER 9

STACI'S BODY WAS WARM, inside and out. Though a lot had to do with the fire and food, a good deal of the warmth had to do with the fact she was practically naked beneath the blanket. She still wore her bra and panties, but that didn't stop her from imagining losing them as well.

How could she be having lustful thoughts about this stranger she barely knew? Weren't most relationships grounded in knowing a person for a period longer than a couple of days? She was a woman of science. However, nothing about what she was feeling had anything to do with science.

She stood beside him in front of the fire, fighting an incredible urge to drop her blanket and offer herself to him. She'd never felt that way with Trevor. Yes, they'd had sex, though she'd never wanted to strip in front of him and ask him to make love to her.

What kept her from throwing herself at Cole was the terrifying fear of rejection. Yeah, he'd kissed her, and it had been so good, but that didn't mean he wanted to make love to her.

They were on the run from people who wanted to hurt them, maybe even kill them. Yet she was thinking about getting naked with her rescuer. She should be cowering in a corner. Instead, she was standing next to the man who had her blood burning through her veins.

"We should probably sleep," Cole said.

"Yes, we should," Staci agreed, yet made no move to comply. "Aren't your clothes still damp?"

Cole ran his fingers down the front of his jeans. "Just a little."

Staci's heart raced, and she turned toward Cole. "My things should be dry soon. Here, you take the blanket." She let the blanket fall down to her waist and then unwrapped it from her body and handed it to him. She couldn't believe she was being so brazen.

He took the blanket automatically. His gaze swept over her body, a frown creasing his brow. "Should I read more into this than you just handing over a blanket?"

Staci bit her bottom lip as heat rose to her neck and into her cheeks. She lifted her chin and inhaled, the air filling her lungs making her breasts rise. She refused to cover herself. This was who she was. If he wanted her, he would know what he was getting, not be blinded by darkness in a cell inside a mountain. "What do you want my action to mean?"

He tossed the blanket onto the mattress and raised his hands to her cheeks. "It's insane to believe that you would want to make love with me in this shack in the middle of a valley of crazy people. But as ridiculous as it might seem, making love with you makes the most sense of anything that has happened since I arrived in Glory Valley."

Her heart swelled, and the knot in her gut eased to be replaced by heat coiling at her core. She let go of a breath she didn't realize she'd been holding in a nervous laugh. "You want to?"

He grinned. "More than I want to breathe at this moment." He took another step closer to her and bent to brush his lips across hers in a feather-like kiss. "I've dreamed of making love to you since before I even knew what you looked like. Our late-night conversations in the dark, listening to you talk, tied me in knots. I couldn't believe that I could be so captivated simply by a woman's voice. But it wasn't just because it was a woman's voice; it was your voice."

"You made me feel safe," she said with a laugh. "Even when I was locked in that black abyss of a cell."

He tipped her head back and stared down into her eyes, the firelight making her red hair glow like shiny copper. "Is it wrong to want you so much? You're my client. I'm the hired help. I'd be taking advantage of you."

Staci ran her hands up his muscular chest and back down to the hem of his shirt. "The way I see it, I'd be taking advantage of you. You don't have to do this," she said as she lifted his shirt up his torso.

He took over, dragged the shirt over his head and tossed it onto the table.

Finally, she was able to touch the skin stretched tightly over the hardness of his muscles. She trailed her fingers across that broad chest, pausing to circle the hard brown nipples. Then she leaned down and flicked one with the tip of her tongue.

He inhaled sharply.

Staci looked up with a frown. "Does that hurt?"

"Oh, sweetheart, no."

Her frown deepened. "Tickle?"

He gathered her in his arms chest. "No, it's making me want to move this a little faster."

A smile curled her lips as a rush of power surged through her. She reached for the button of his jeans and flicked it open. Then she lowered the zipper slowly.

His cock sprung out.

She cupped him in her hand, amazed at how thick and hard he was already. Her channel clenched and drenched with cream. "Yes, let's move this along a little faster."

He ran his hands down the length of her throat

and threw them across the curve of her shoulders. He stopped there and frowned. "We can't do this."

She stared up into his eyes. "Why not? I want this. If you want it, too, we're two consenting single adults. What's stopping us? Well, besides the potential of someone walking through that door and pointing a gun at us…nothing should keep this from happening."

"I don't have protection," he stated.

"Oh." Staci tried to think of a way around that little issue. "That does complicate things." She looked up into his eyes. "Do you ever want another child?" she asked. "Not that another child could take the place of the one you lost. I'm sorry. When I get nervous, I talk too much."

He kissed her lips, claiming her mouth in a long, toe-curling kiss that left her breathless and wanting so much more. When he finally raised his head, she leaned her forehead against his chest. "I don't suppose the kids are smart enough to keep protection handy…?" She leaned back and looked around the room.

"There has to be some. Rebecca's too smart and ambitious to let herself get pregnant at fifteen. Look." She went through the tins and containers on the shelves with no luck.

Cole flipped the folded mattress so that it lay flat on the wooden bed frame. A couple of pillows had been hidden inside the fold. Cole lifted one and shook it. A small box fell to the floor. Cole reached for it and read the package contents. "You were right. Rebecca is smart and doesn't want an unplanned pregnancy." He held up the package. "We're back in business if it's what you still want."

She reached for the box, pulled out a small packet and tossed the box with the remainder of its contents onto the table. "I don't have a watch, and the clouds are making it difficult to gauge how much longer until morning. Let's get this party started."

Cole laughed out loud, swept her up in his arms and deposited her on the mattress. He kicked off his shoes, shucked his jeans and joined her.

He pressed kisses to her forehead, eyelids, cheeks, and lips. When Staci thought he might not ever get to the point, he moved down her neck to the pulse beating at the base. Then he crossed over her collar-bone and lower to capture her nipple through the lace fabric of her bra.

Staci sat up, unclipped her bra and let the straps slide down her shoulders. Lying back, she shimmied out of her panties and lay naked against the thin mattress.

Cole leaned to the side on one elbow and smiled down at her, his gaze sweeping across her, lingering on the swells of her breasts and the juncture of her thighs. The look of hunger in his eyes made her reach out, slip her arm around his neck and pull him down to her, guiding his mouth to one nipple already beaded in a tight little nub.

He sucked the breast into his mouth and pulled. Then he flicked his tongue across the tip and switched to the other breast.

Staci writhed beneath the onslaught of his kisses, nips and tonguing. Her fingers wove into his black hair, urging him even lower.

His mouth skimmed over her ribs and lower still until he arrived at the tuft of hair over her sex.

Cole positioned himself between her legs and parted her folds, thumbing the narrow strip of flesh inside.

Sensations rocketed through her body. When he touched her there again with his thumb, she raised her knees and dug her heels into the mattress.

When he touched her there with the tip of his tongue, Staci cried out.

He raised his head. "Hurt?"

"No!" she gasped. "Yes. Oh, so good. Please, do it again."

He tongued her clit again, settling in to take her all the way.

The tension inside her built to a peak. When he slid his fingers into her channel at the same time as he flicked her nubbin, she thought she would die with the overwhelming surge of desire that pushed her up and over the edge.

Her release came in waves, washing over her

again and again until she floated back to earth and lay against the mattress for a few long seconds. It wasn't enough; she wanted to feel him inside, connected, complete.

With her fingers wound tightly in his hair, she tugged and urged him to climb up her body.

Propped on his hands, leaning over her body, he stared into her eyes. He leaned back, applied the condom and settled between her legs. "It's not too late to say no."

"Don't start now," she cried. "I want you inside me…now."

His cock nudging her entrance.

Staci gripped his buttocks and urged him to take her.

He slid in, her channel slick with her juices, easing his path. His shaft filled her completely, pushing all the way to the back. For a long moment, he remained still, allowing her body time to accommodate his girth.

Then, moving slowly, he pumped in and out in a steady rhythm.

Staci wanted more. Gripping his buttocks in her hands, she increased the speed until he rocked their bodies.

She raised her hips, meeting him thrust for thrust until he slammed into her one last time and held steady, his body tense, his cock throbbing inside her.

When he lay on the narrow bed beside her, he gathered her in his arms and held her.

Everything about making love with Cole felt right. If she could control the future, Staci would live the rest of her life wrapped in his arms. With him, she could be her normal awkward self and feel good about it.

"Where do we go from here?" she whispered with her lips pressed to his chest.

"Away from this valley," he said, the sound reverberating against her ear.

Sleep pulled at her, dragging her into the dark as she closed her heavy eyes. "After we leave Glory Valley, will we ever see each other again?" she asked.

"Wild horses couldn't keep me away," he whispered.

With a smile on her face, Staci drifted into an exhausted sleep, knowing Cole would give whatever it took to get them to safety. Hopefully, that wouldn't include giving his life.

COLE LAY AWAKE LONG after Staci succumbed to sleep. He liked holding her in his arms. She was so very different from Lisa. He couldn't compare them. Lisa had had blond hair and blue eyes. Staci was a redhead with hazel eyes. Lisa had possessed an innate confidence and fierce independence. Staci had to work at independence and confidence, and yet she was brilliant and very good at what she did as a doctor.

Lisa had been content to stay home and raise their children.

Staci had so much love in her heart for others she chose to give back, even when it placed her in danger.

They were both amazing women in their own right. He'd love Lisa with all his heart. Could he open his heart to love Staci? Would it be disloyal to Lisa to fall in love again and live his life to the fullest? Was it fair to Lisa and Tyler's memory to start over with another woman and possibly another child?

He might not have a choice in the matter. Cole suspected he was already falling in love with the beautiful, brilliantly talented doctor. If that was what he was feeling, would he be enough for her? Didn't she deserve a man of equal intelligence and education? He was good at what he did. Was it enough?

He drifted to sleep, holding onto the woman, savoring the time he had with her, not knowing what the future might hold for them or whether they were destined to be together or apart.

He really wanted more time with her either way. Getting out of Glory Valley was the first obstacle, and he had some ideas on how to do that. He'd run them by her when he woke.

.   .   .

SEVERAL HOURS LATER, Cole woke. He lay for a while, loving the warmth of Staci's naked body against his. If he'd thought they had time, he'd wake her and make love with her again. Without a watch or clock, he had no idea what time it was or how soon sunrise would happen. He wanted to be ready to go in the gray light of dawn, well before sunup.

He slipped his arm out from under her body and tucked the blanket around her. The fire had died down to embers. Cole needed to bank it completely before the sun came up to keep smoke from escaping through the chimney. The shack had to appear deserted to maintain Rebecca's secret hideaway and their current position.

After he stirred and separated the embers,

Cole slipped into his clothes and shoes and turned to Staci.

With barely any light from the fire, he couldn't make out her expression. He could tell her eyes were open.

She lay on her side, her hand beneath her cheek.

He smiled. "Sleep okay?"

She nodded. "Any regrets?"

Cole dipped his head once. "One."

She cocked her eyebrow. "Only one?"

He shrugged. "I have more than one regret."

Her lips turned downward. "I'm sorry to hear that."

"Don't be. One regret is that the night wasn't

longer to spend more time with you in my arms," he said. "Another regret is that our first time wasn't in a bed of roses instead of a hard mattress in a cold shack in crazy valley." He sat on the edge of the bed and stroked the hair back from her face. "The peas in the kettle are still warm. Let's eat, then I'll tell you about my plan."

"You have a plan?" Her eyebrows rose, and she sat up, the blanket falling down around her waist.

Cole moaned. "Do you know how hard it is to keep from making love with you right now?"

"What's holding you back, soldier?" she asked.

"Time," he said. "I want to get an early start."

She reached for his hand and brought it up to cup her breast. "Are you sure we don't have time? We can skip the foreplay."

"You tempt me, woman," he growled and bent to suck her nipple into his mouth. When he straightened, he sighed. "As much as I'd like to lay in bed all morning with you. We need to move on. I want to sneak into town, see if we can commandeer some weapons and a set of wheels. We have a better chance of blowing past a roadblock in a vehicle versus on foot."

"Do you know how to hotwire a car?" Staci asked.

"No, but how hard could it be?"

Her lips twisted. "A lot harder than you think…?"

"Guess we'll find out." He tossed her clothes to

her and stood back. "I'd like to leave in ten minutes. Will you be ready?"

Staci laughed. "Since I don't have a brush, makeup or clean clothes, I'll be ready in one." She swung her legs over the side of the mattress and stood, naked, beautiful and too tempting for Cole.

"Woman, do you have any idea what you do to me?"

Her smile was wickedly teasing. "I have an idea."

He pulled her into his arms and crushed her lips with his in a kiss that would have to suffice for the moment. His hands slid down her back to cup her ass, and then he smacked her bottom and stepped back. "Promise me something."

Her brow wrinkled. "What?"

"When we're back in the real world, we won't be awkward. This wasn't just a sex-against-the-wall kind of moment or a figment of my imagination."

She cupped his cheek in the palm of her hand. "Sweetheart, in all this madness, you're the only real thing that's kept me going."

He covered her hand on his cheek. "Same. And it's more than that. You've given me hope."

"How so?"

"Hope for a brighter future where I'm not buried in a dark past, filled with regret."

She leaned up on her toes and brushed her lips across his. "Does this mean we'll see each other again?" She gave him a tremulous smile. "Please say yes."

He wrapped his arms around her naked body and held her close, loving the feel of her against him. "Yes. Yes. And hell yes."

"Good. I'm not good at goodbyes."

For a long moment, they stood in each other's arms.

Finally, Cole set her to arm's length. "Get dressed, we need to get out of this valley so we can pick up where we left off."

He stirred the ashes in the fireplace to make sure no embers remained hot and producing smoke. Then he went to the door and peered out. The clouds had cleared, revealing a starlit sky. They'd have no trouble navigating the valley as long as the sky remained clear. With the absence of clouds, there was nothing to hold in the earth's heat. The temperatures had dropped, glazing the ground with frost. The valley lay in darkness, the inhabitants still asleep. Cole hoped they stayed that way long enough for them to sneak into the town and acquire what they'd need to make a run for it through the pass.

Staci dressed quickly and pulled on her shoes and jacket. When she was ready, she joined him near the door.

They'd just stepped out of the shack when a horse burst through the brush along the creek and raced toward them, its rider leaning low over its neck.

Cole and Staci slipped back through the shack's door and closed it to a crack until they could ascertain the identity of the rider.

The horse didn't slow, heading directly for the shack at a dangerous speed.

Just when Cole thought the horse would run right into the structure, the rider pulled back on the reins so hard the animal skidded to a stop and reared in protest.

Once its hooves hit the ground, the rider slid from the saddle and raced for the shack.

Cole opened the door, and Rebecca Severson fell through it, breathing hard, her dark hair wild and tangled, and her eyes red-rimmed from crying.

Staci wrapped her in her arms. "Hey, sweetie, what's wrong?"

"It's Dalton." Rebecca bent over, her shoulders shaking with the force of her sobs. She swallowed hard and forced herself to go on. "They've taken him. My father and Ezekiel went to the Jensen's' house where he's been staying and loaded him in the truck. They drove up the mountain toward the mine. I'm afraid for him. I'm afraid of what my father will do with Dalton, his father and the others."

"Why?" Staci asked. "What do you know?"

"Only what I overheard them talking about last night. They said something about getting rid of the evidence." She looked up through her tears. "I'm afraid the evidence is the people they've held hostage."

Cole touched the girl's arm. "Are the phones working?"

She frowned. "I think so. My parents have one in their bedroom."

"Are you able to get to it and place a call?" Cole asked.

"I'm not allowed in their bedroom," Rebecca said. "They keep it locked. "We're not allowed to use the phones. It's one of the rules. My friend did once, her father whipped her with a horsewhip."

"And I'm sure you're not supposed to be meeting a boy in a shack in a field." Staci gave the girl a gentle smile.

Rebecca lifted her head, her jaw tightening. "I'll get in."

Cole gripped Rebecca's arms and stared into her eyes. "When you get to a phone, call 9-1-1. Tell them where you are, and that people have been taken hostage by armed men."

"They'll kill me if I do that," Rebecca whispered.

"You have to take that chance and break the rule if you want to save Dalton," Staci said.

"Do they still have people guarding the pass?" Cole asked.

Rebecca nodded. "They're armed with rifles and shotguns. It takes too long for anyone to get to us.

Dalton and his father might not have long enough for help to get here."

"After your call 9-1-1, I want you to call Jake Cogburn," Cole said. He took a charred stick from the fireplace and drew the number on Rebecca's arm. "Memorize the number. The charcoal won't last. Tell Jake what's happening. He'll send help as well."

The girl nodded.

Cole was afraid they were asking too much of the frightened teen. However, they had no choice. They needed help to free the prisoners and save Dalton.

"Rebecca, it would help if we had weapons and a vehicle," Cole said. "Is there any way we can get our hands on those?"

Rebecca's eyes rounded. "My father keeps his guns in a box in the barn behind our house. It has a lock on it."

Cole shot a glance to Staci. "A padlock?"

The girl nodded, a frown creasing her forehead. "I don't have the key."

"We'll handle the lock while you place the phone calls," Staci said.

"My father has an old truck in the barn he only uses when they haul hay from the fields. It's not the best, but it works."

"The keys?" Cole asked.

Rebecca smiled. "In the truck. It's that ugly, no one would want to take it."

"It'll be light soon. We need to get to your house before the sun rises," Cole said.

"You can ride back with me on my horse," she said.

Staci frowned. "Will it be too much with the three of us?"

She shook her head. "Little Joe is strong. He pulls a heavy plow during planting season. He can handle it."

Since Cole was the biggest, he would ride in the saddle. He quickly adjusted the stirrups for his legs and swung up into the saddle.

Staci was next. She placed her foot on top of Cole's and, with his help, swung up behind the saddle and held on around his waist. Rebecca mounted behind Staci.

With a gentle nudge from Cole's heels, Little Joe took off at a gentle gallop across the field.

Rebecca guided them through the valley to the outskirts of the old mining town.

They dismounted, tied the horse to a tree and hurried around the backs of the buildings and homes until they arrived at the Seversons' house.

A light shone from a room on the ground floor. Through the window, Cole could see Elizabeth moving around.

"My mother is in the kitchen, probably cooking breakfast. While she's busy, I'll make those calls." She nodded toward the shed behind the house. "Be careful, the barn is visible from the kitchen."

"You be careful." Staci hugged the girl.

"I'll make those calls if I have to lock myself in my parent's room long enough to get through."

"Thank you," Cole said. "Now, go. We don't have much time."

"In the barn, you'll find a flashlight on the wall to the left of the door and tools to help you with the lock." Rebecca turned toward her house, climbed up a tree and slipped through an upstairs window.

Cole shook his head. "She's a rebel."

Staci smiled in the light from the fading stars. "I hope we can help her."

"We will." Cole slipped through the shadows to the barn.

Time was passing too fast. They had to get up the mountain to the mine and keep Cyrus and Ezekiel from disposing of the *evidence*.

CHAPTER 10

STACI FOLLOWED Cole as he entered the barn. Her heart pounded, and she had a hard time breathing normally. The altitude had little to do with her struggle. Breaking and entering to steal weapons and a vehicle had more impact on her ability to draw a breath. She was a rule-follower by nature. Never had she ever broken a law.

Desperate times called for desperate measures. Lives depended on their ability to defend those being exploited.

Once inside the barn with the door closed behind them, Cole grabbed the flashlight from the wall, clicked it on and shined it around the space. He paused when the light landed on a wooden cabinet against the side wall. "That has to be his gun cabinet," he whispered.

"Do we need to find a file for the lock?" Staci asked.

He shined the light at a wall with every tool imaginable hanging from hooks on a pegboard.

"Maybe," he said, still looking.

Staci spotted a pair of bolt cutters leaning against the wall, grabbed them and held them up. "How about this?"

Cole grinned, took the bolt cutters, handed her the flashlight and kissed her. "You're amazing."

Her heart swelled at his words. Trevor had never spoken to her like that. Why had she ever been interested in him? He was cold and distant whereas Cole was warm-hearted and hot-blooded. Memories of the night before washed over her, making her wish they were back in that shack, making love, not sneaking around someone else's barn, breaking laws.

She led the way to the gun cabinet and held the flashlight while Cole cut the padlock. Inside the box was an array of weapons that shocked Staci. For a community that believed in living off the land as much as possible, their leader had guns. Powerful guns. Guns that weren't meant for hunting food.

"Two AR 15s, various rifles..." Cole whistled softly.

"What?" Staci asked.

"He's got a .338 Lapua," Cole spoke reverently.

"What's a Lapua?" Staci asked.

"One of the best long-range sniper rifles money

can buy." Cole snagged one of the rifles that looked like something soldiers carried.

"Is that the Lapua?" Staci asked.

"No," he said. "This is an AR15, much like the M4A1 rifles we use in Delta Force." He pocketed several magazines full of bullets and turned to Staci. "Do you want a gun?"

She shook her head. "Not unless it's a taser."

He grinned. "You're in luck. He has several." He handed her a belt. "Wear that."

While she buckled the belt, he grabbed a gun like those Ezekiel and Cyrus wore in the mines. "Why don't they carry guns with bullets when dealing with the prisoners?" she asked. "Not that I want them to."

"They can't use bullets in the mines," Cole said. "The walls are solid rock. The bullets would bounce off the rocks and might ricochet back at the shooter."

She nodded, took the taser Cole handed her and clipped it to the belt. "Makes sense."

Cole turned toward an old truck that probably dated back to the 1960s. At one time, it had been red and white. Now it was rust and white, the upholstery long since deteriorated.

"She wasn't kidding about it being ugly," Staci said.

"Doesn't matter what it looks like as long as it runs." He laid the AR15 across the bench seat and slipped behind the wheel.

"I'll get the door," Staci said.

Cole reached for the key which, as Rebecca had indicated, was in the ignition. He turned the key and the engine turned over several times then putted into silence.

After several pumps on the accelerator, Cole turned the key again. This time the engine rolled over and roared to life.

Loud enough to wake anyone sleeping and to alert Elizabeth to trouble in the barn.

Staci opened the barn doors and ran for the passenger door of the old truck. When she pulled on the door handle, nothing happened. Cole leaned across and tried to open it from the inside. It was a no-go.

Using the crank handle, Cole rolled down the window. "Climb through or come around to my side."

Staci stared at the window. "I don't know if I can climb through."

Cole's head came up, and he stared toward the house. "Hell, we've got company. Either get in through the window or ride in the truck bed."

Staci followed his gaze.

Elizabeth charged out of the kitchen, headed their way and carrying a shotgun.

With no other choice, Staci climbed up the truck's wheel, rolled over the side wall of the truck and dropped into the truck bed.

As she landed, Cole hit the accelerator, shooting them forward and through the barn door.

She managed to get to her knees and poke her head over the rim of the truck bed.

Cole rounded the side of the house, heading for the road.

Elizabeth raised her shotgun and aimed at the truck.

Staci dropped down into the truck bed as the gun went off.

The windshield shattered, and Cole swerved.

"Oh, God. Cole!" she screamed.

"I'm all right," he responded. "What about you?"

"Alive," she said.

As he reached Main Street, someone leaped off the Seversons' front porch and raced toward the truck.

Rebecca hopped onto the back bumper and dove into the truck bed seconds before Cole pressed the accelerator to the floor, heading for the mine.

Staci helped the girl to a kneeling position. "Rebecca, you can't come with us, it's too dangerous."

"I did what you asked. I made the two calls." Her lips pressed into a tight line. "Maybe I can help. Maybe my father will listen to me." She didn't look like she believed her own words. "I couldn't stay back. Not when it's my family causing harm. I had to come."

"You are not responsible for your father's actions."

"My silence about what's been going on makes me just as guilty," she said. "I will not forgive myself if one of those men, or Dalton, are harmed or killed."

"What did the 9-1-1 operator say?" Staci asked.

"They're sending someone out. They told me to go somewhere safe until they get here." Rebecca laughed. "No way. I have to help."

"What about the other number Cole gave you?"

"I got a man named Jake. He said their team is already on their way. ETA ten minutes." She grimaced. "What is ETA?"

"Estimated time of arrival," Staci said, daring to hope ten minutes was right. Surely, they could hold off the end of the world for ten lousy minutes.

Staci was not at all sure what they'd do when they got to the mine. The odds would be stacked against them, at least four to one, if not worse.

Hopefully, they could at least delay Cyrus and Ezekiel from harming the prisoners until help arrived. Although, one soldier with a rifle against a dozen men…?

Her heart pinched tightly in her chest. This could end badly. Especially, if bullets started flying.

They reached the end of the pavement and bumped along the rutted, gravel road leading up to the mine. If the valley men were at the mine building, they would see them coming. The familiar truck might confuse them long enough for Cole and Staci

165

to get into a good position to defend themselves. If they could keep them occupied…

For how long?

Staci thought about the number of magazines full of bullets Cole had slipped into his pockets and shook her head.

She didn't even have her satchel with what few medical supplies she had left since arriving in Glory Valley. If Cole was hurt, she could do little to help.

The best-case scenario would be to try to talk the valley men out of whatever dastardly thing they had in mind for their prisoners and hope she and Cole weren't recaptured and added to their grisly plans.

She glanced over at Rebecca, and her heart ached for the girl. To know her father was involved in imprisoning men, and could potentially kill them, had to be a tough pill to swallow. Being forced to marry someone she didn't love at the tender age of sixteen was the least of her current worries.

"When we get there, we need to stay down," Staci said. "Cole is a trained warrior. He's our best chance for delaying whatever your father and Ezekiel have in mind until help arrives. If we get in his way, we might jeopardize his success."

Rebecca nodded. "I hope that I can talk some sense into my father. He can't seriously consider disposing of four people like so much trash. He's an asshole and stuck in the past, but he's not a killer." Her brow twisted. "At least, I hope he's not." She clutched Staci's hands. "We can't let him hurt those people."

"He's already hurt them by keeping them prisoner in that tunnel and forcing them to work in the mines," Staci reminded the teen. "Not to mention using the cattle prods and tasers on them. We might not be able to reason with him. At this point, he's broken laws by imprisoning people, including me. He might think he's got to get rid of these people so there's no one to talk about his crimes."

Rebecca stared ahead at the mine building ahead. "The people of the valley won't say anything. He's had them cowed for so long, they'll keep their mouths shut. But it's not just our people now. You and Cole could tell the authorities about what they've done." Her eyes widened. "And you're walking right into it. They'll take this opportunity to add you to the number of people they're disposing of." Her eyes filled. "I've led you right into a trap. I'm so sorry. I shouldn't have told you or gotten you involved."

Staci squeezed her hands. "No, you had to. We were the only people you could trust to help. You have a kind heart and couldn't let them harm Dalton or the others."

"If I'd had a kind heart, I would've gone to the authorities sooner," Rebecca said.

"You can't blame yourself. It serves no purpose. And we're here. How do we get around to the tunnel where they house the prisoners?"

Rebecca leaned out the side of the truck bed and yelled to Cole. "Drive around to the left of the building and drive along the side of the mountain."

Staci dragged her back down into the bed of the truck. "It might be best if they don't know we're here yet. Stay down below the sides of the truck bed.

Staci and Rebecca hunkered low, barely peeking their heads over the rim as the truck rounded the mine building and the side of the mountain.

They had to rise up enough to see through the front windshield.

Staci's breath caught, and her blood ran cold.

More than a dozen men stood outside the entrance to the tunnel.

Cyrus held Dalton's arm.

The boy's wrists had been bound with zip-ties, and he was struggling to free himself from the older man's hold.

Rebecca gasped and dove for the side of the truck.

Staci just caught her to keep her from jumping out. "Let Cole handle this. Again, if we get involved, Cole will lose focus. Loss of focus could get him killed, and no one would be able to help keep the others alive until the authorities or Cole's team arrives."

Rebecca shook with the force of her anger. "How could he do this?"

The valley men carried rifles and shotguns and

had spread out, creating a semi-circle perimeter around the entrance to the tunnel.

Ezekiel had Dalton's other arm and was struggling to keep his hold on the young man.

Ezekiel hit the boy with his cattle prod.

Dalton yelped and settled down. "You can't do this. You're animals to treat people the way you're treating my father. You won't get away with this."

As the ground leveled off, Cole sped up.

"Hold on!" he yelled out the window.

Staci and Rebecca held onto the sides of the truck bed and braced themselves.

The men standing around turned to watch the speeding truck coming at them. Just as some raised their weapons, Cole slammed on the brakes and brought the truck to a skidding halt, turning it at a diagonal to place the front right bumper and the engine between him and the men holding guns.

He leaped out of the truck with the AR15, slammed the door closed and braced his weapon over the hood and engine. "Cyrus Severson, let go of the boy!"

COLE HESITATED over who to aim the AR 15 at, Cyrus or Ezekiel. As much as he despised Ezekiel, Cyrus was in charge. He couldn't fire anyway, not as long as they held the teen so close. He had no doubt they

169

would use the kid as a human shield to protect their own asses.

"Or what?" Cyrus called out. "Or you'll start shooting?" He waved a hand at the men who'd dropped to the ground and were now aiming at Cole. "Are you going to shoot every man out here?"

"I don't want to shoot anyone. Let the boy go and the people you've held as prisoners," Cole said. "It's over."

"What's over?" Cyrus demanded.

"The authorities are on their way. They will arrest you. Now, whether it's for false imprisonment or murder is up to you."

"They won't arrest me for either," Cyrus said. "Who have I imprisoned? Who will be left to tell?"

"I will," Cole said.

Out of the corner of his eye, Cole saw Rebecca Severson push up to stand in the back of the truck. "And I will," she shouted. "This is wrong, Father. You have to set those men free."

Her father glared at Rebecca. "You think I didn't know you were sneaking out at night to see this punk? After all I've done for you. For this community. For our way of life. You'd turn on me?"

Rebecca's chin lifted. "What you're doing is wrong. You can't hold people hostage and make them work your mine. It's wrong."

"Shut up, girl. You're dead to me. You are no longer a member of this family or our people."

"Good!" she yelled. "I was leaving anyway. I refused to be told who I will marry and at what age. I want to live my own life, make my own choices, not marry at sixteen and have babies to populate a dying town. That's your dream, not mine. You can keep it."

"You can go to hell with the outsiders," her father said. He turned to his men. "There is only one man with a gun. We are over a dozen. Take him."

"Don't listen to him!" Cole said. "If you attack me, you're committing a crime. You're already accessories to the crime of false imprisonment. Do you want to add murder to your rap sheets and the number of years you'll spend in jail?"

"Don't listen to him," Ezekiel said. "He would change the way we live, bring in more outsiders and pollute the minds of our wives and children. We can't let that happen. Our valley has been in our families for over a century. We've raised our children according to our values, not someone else's. Others will destroy what we've worked hard to preserve."

"Maybe it was already crumbling from within," Rebecca said. "I heard what Dr. Miller said. By only marrying within our community, we're ruining our future and the futures of the children." Rebecca waved her hand toward one of the men. "Mr. Jones, how many miscarriages did your wife have before little Bethany? And hasn't Bethany had issues since she was born?"

"That could happen to anyone," Ezekiel countered.

Rebecca glared at the man. "Well, it's happening more and more. Just about every woman has had at least one miscarriage, if not more. And how many of the babies are born with some abnormality? We can't keep doing this to our people."

"She's right." Staci stood tall beside Rebecca. "There is a startling number of abnormalities in the children of Glory Valley that could be a result of inbreeding. The gene pool isn't large enough to sustain a healthy population."

"That will be enough," Cyrus commanded.

Rebecca shrank back at his tone, and then came back with, "No! It's not enough."

Cyrus waved toward his men. "Take them," he ordered. Then he turned and walked toward the tunnel. Ezekiel whipped around, placing Dalton in front of him as a shield and backed toward the tunnel. Cyrus pulled open the iron door and stepped inside. Ezekiel dragged Dalton in with him.

Cole couldn't take the shot. If he missed, he'd hit the kid.

"No! Rebecca shouted. "You can't let them do this!"

She tried to jump from the truck, but Staci held her back.

Cole had his own problems to contend with. More than a dozen men were heading his way, weapons pointed at him. "I don't want to shoot any of you. But I will if you don't back off and let us save those people Cyrus plans to kill."

His words did nothing to stop them from coming toward him. "Damn, and I thought I was done killing when I left the Army." He raised his rifle to his shoulder and fired at the ground in front of the man closest to him.

The man backed up a step then raised his rifle and fired at Cole. His bullet hit somewhere on the front of the truck.

"Ladies," Cole yelled. "Get down and stay down!"

The men came at him.

Cole did not want to kill them. These men were farmers with families. He couldn't help but think of Dusty's wife and children, having to go through life without their father.

Then again, if he didn't do something, they'd overrun his position and take the women.

He aimed at the man closest to him and laid his finger on the trigger. He was just about to pull the trigger when the thump of rotor blades filled the sky. A UH1H Huey helicopter burst over the top of the mountain and hovered a hundred feet in the air.

Five ropes dropped from the aircraft like so many snakes, twisting and swirling in the blast from the blades.

Five men, wearing body armor, helmets and military-grade rifles fast-roped to the ground.

The men who had been advancing on Cole's position stopped to stare at the Huey, a throwback to the Vietnam War era. They probably didn't know the helicopter had been retired from military use back in 2014.

Cole almost laughed at their astonishment and confusion. With his team coming in from another direction and the valley men's attention on them, he had the opportunity to race into the tunnel and stop Cyrus and Ezekiel from shoving the prisoners over the edge of a deep vertical shaft.

Leaving the cover of the old pickup, Cole ran toward the tunnel entrance.

He didn't get there because two big men stepped into his path. One swung a fist and hit him square in the jaw, knocking him backward.

Cole staggered a few steps, and then came back swinging. He hit the man who'd hit him in the belly. When he bent over, Cole planted an uppercut to the man's jaw.

By then another man stepped into the fray, grabbed Cole's arm and yanked him backward.

Out of the corner of his eye, he could see the Brotherhood Protectors converging on the valley men. Other than two shots initially fired, the men had chosen to fight with their fists.

With the odds still two or three to one, he'd have to fight his way through the men to get to the prisoners. He hoped he'd get there in time, and that the prisoners would put up a fight. Their odds were better with only Cyrus and Ezekiel to contend with.

Unfortunately, the prisoners weren't trained combatants. The two valley men had their tasers and could render their hostages immobile, which would make it more difficult for the valley men to get them to the edge of anything.

Cole focused on the men in front of him first.

CHAPTER 11

"No!" Rebecca struggled to break Staci's hold on her arm. "Let go! They took Dalton in there. We have to help."

After the first rounds were fired, Staci had done her best to keep Rebecca down. Her arm ached from the effort.

When the helicopter popped up over the top of the mountain, Staci wanted to stand up and cheer.

The fight wasn't over, but the cavalry had arrived. As the aircraft hovered above them, she counted five men sliding down ropes to the ground. Her gaze went back to the helicopter, expecting at least five more. No one else stepped out and slid down the ropes. Was that all the help they were getting? Would it be enough? They were still outnumbered.

As soon as Cole's team merged with the valley men, she felt a little more confident they would win the battle. The men quickly proved they were in better shape and had better skills than the farmers who'd never fought in a war. And she was glad both sides hadn't resorted to more bullets. It was bad enough they were smashing each other's faces.

With all the would-be rescuers occupied, no one had made it to the tunnel to rescue the prisoners.

"We can't wait for your man to free up," Rebecca said. "We have to help Dalton and the others before it's too late." She jerked her arm from Staci's grasp. "I'm going in."

The teen vaulted over the side of the truck bed and raced toward the iron door on the side of the mountain.

"Rebecca!" Staci leaped from the truck and ran after the girl, dodging between fighting men and leaping over the ones who lay unconscious on the ground.

Ahead of her, Rebecca pushed back the heavy iron door and ran into the dark tunnel.

Staci's heart jumped into her throat as she entered that dark abyss that had seemed to suck the very life out of her. Having escaped it once, she'd never wanted to return. Now, here she was, running back into the very mouth of hell.

Inside the tunnel, the only light was what shone in from the door and the light from Cyrus's and Ezekiel's headlamps halfway down the line of cells. Between them, they were struggling with Dalton. Cyrus held him under his arms, and Ezekiel fought to keep a grip on his ankles. The teen kicked and twisted, fighting for his life.

Rebecca rushed her father. "Let go of him!" She pounded on his back with her fists.

When he didn't release the boy, Rebecca jumped on his back, grabbed his hair and pulled as hard as she could.

"Damn you," her father yelled. Releasing his hold on Dalton, he reached behind him, dragged his daughter off his back and threw her to the ground.

She sprang up and went at him again, clawing at his face. "I hate you!" she screamed. "I hate you, and hope you rot in hell!"

Cyrus's face turned a deep ruddy red. He backhanded his daughter, sending her flying backward. She hit the rock wall and slid to the ground.

"Don't hurt her," Staci yelled. "She's your daughter." Staci ran toward the man, ducked her shoulder and rammed into him, pushing him back until he slammed into the metal bars of the cell where she'd spent so many hours in the blackness.

Ezekiel left Dalton on the ground and ran toward Staci.

She pulled the taser from the clip and barely had time to raise it when he plowed into her.

She pulled the trigger as she fell backward, landing on her ass.

Ezekiel fell on top of her, his body a deadweight, his muscles unresponsive.

Staci rolled him to the side and pushed to her feet.

Rebecca moaned and stirred where she'd fallen against the wall.

Staci would have helped her up, but she was more worried about the teen's father.

Where was Cyrus?

As Staci spun toward the door to the tunnel, an arm clamped around her neck, bringing her up short.

"We were doing just fine until you showed up," Cyrus growled in her ear. "Now you've destroyed us. Ruined our lives and forced me to do something I never would've done otherwise." He yanked her around and marched her deeper into the tunnel.

The more she struggled, the more he tightened his hold around her neck until she felt light-headed, and even with the headlamp Cyrus wore darkness surrounded her.

Was this it? Would she die at the bottom of a mine shaft? In the dark. Alone.

A surge of determination rose up inside her.

Hell no. She would not die. Not now. Not here.

Staci dug her heels into the hard rock floor of the tunnel, bringing her and Cyrus to a halt.

Cocking her elbow, she drove it as hard as she could into Cyrus's midsection.

He grunted, and his arm loosened slightly.

Staci turned her head, pushed his arm up and

dropped out of his hold. On her way down, she elbowed him in the nuts, dove around his legs, rolled and sprang to her feet.

She had taken only three steps when a hand sank into her hair and jerked her backward so hard, her feet flew out from under her.

With his hand still tangled in her hair, Cyrus dragged her across the floor.

She twisted and rolled, but he wouldn't let go, and she couldn't rise to her feet or reach him to make him stop. She'd failed, and now she would die.

He must have been losing his touch or these farmers had rock-solid jaws and guts. Cole swung his bruised knuckles once more, knocking his third valley man to the ground.

The other Brotherhood Protectors were quickly putting an end to the fight.

Jake yelled, "Drop your weapons and get down on your knees!"

The valley men laid down their weapons, raised their hands and admitted defeat, their faces bruised and bloody.

Cole crossed to Jake and Thorn, never happier to see the men of his new team. "Your timing perfect."

Thorn chuckled. "I figured you might need some

help since you didn't show up at our designated time and location."

Jake held out his hand. "I'd been working on a training exercise for our branch of the brotherhood." He tipped his head toward the Huey helicopter hovering above the mountain. "Got a friend who loves flying his relic of a chopper. When Thorn mentioned you might be in trouble, I contacted Jim Bob. He was up for the mission, picked up the team at Lost Valley Ranch and we headed your way. I got a call on my cellphone before I lost signal from a Rebecca that you were in trouble. I was glad we were already on the way."

Rebecca. Staci.

Cole spun toward the truck and ran. He knew before he reached it, they wouldn't be there. After a quick scan of the area, his heart sank into his gut, and he ran for the opening into the tunnel.

"What's wrong?" Thorn caught up with him as he entered the tunnel.

"Got a flashlight?" Cole asked.

"Yup." Thorn pulled a small one from his body armor vest and handed it to Cole.

Cole ran through the tunnel and nearly plowed into Rebecca who was staggering to her feet.

"Where's Staci?"

Rebecca shook her head and swayed. "My father…"

Dalton pushed to his feet. "Cyrus took her deeper into the tunnel."

Cole ran, his heart in his throat, his pulse pounding hard. "Staci!"

"Cole!" she cried faintly. "Help!"

He ran faster.

Ahead, he could see the pale glow of a headlamp moving away from him

"Please," he prayed, "don't die."

Cyrus must have been moving slowly. Cole soon caught up to them.

Cyrus had stopped at the edge of a vertical shaft.

Staci sat at his feet with Cyrus's hand in her hair. She twisted and pushed to her feet.

Cyrus clamped an arm around her neck and turned her toward the drop-off. "One step closer, and she goes over."

Cole froze. "Cyrus, you don't have to do this."

"She destroyed my life. My daughter hates me. Without me, my home and community will crumble and fail. This mine was the only thing keeping us viable. We can't grow enough food to feed all of us. Our men work hard to produce, but it isn't enough. The mine was our only hope to support our people."

"No matter how desperate you are, it's never right to make others suffer," Staci said.

"We had a perfect life," Cyrus said. "And then you came along and ruined it."

"It would've failed anyway. Your people aren't well, and your children are suffering," Cole said.

"She did this to us," Cyrus said and moved another inch toward the shaft.

"Cyrus, if you toss her into the shaft, you won't have any way to get out of here. She's your ticket," Cole said. "You can use her as a hostage and demand anything you want. Her father is rich. He'll pay. You can have him fly you to an island in the Caribbean where you can live out your days in the sun, free of worry. No more snow. No more mines. No more responsibility. Free."

Cyrus stood still for a very long moment. "Is he telling the truth? Is your father rich?"

Staci nodded. "He is. He loves me and would do anything to keep me safe. He would give you whatever you want—if you'd only let me go…alive."

Her voice shook as she teetered on the edge of the shaft.

Cole held his breath, praying Cyrus would go for the trade. Staci for his freedom.

"I'd want to be flown out of this valley before the authorities arrive," Cyrus said.

"Where to?" Cole asked.

"I'll tell the pilot when we're in the air," Cyrus said.

Cole didn't like that. If Cyrus got on that helicopter, the pilot would be at risk. He had to find a way to get Cyrus to release Staci and keep him from getting on the chopper. Until he came up with a brilliant idea, he had to keep Staci alive.

"We can do that," he said. "We have a helicopter hovering outside right now," Cole said. "All you have to do is step outside, climb on board and we can fly you anywhere you want to go."

"Show me." Cyrus swung Staci around to stand in front of him and pressed a knife to her throat. "If I can't get out of here, I have nothing left to lose. Killing her would be my last act of pleasure. So, get me out of this hell hole, and I'll let her live."

Cole breathed for the first time since seeing Staci teetering on the edge of the vertical shaft. Though she wasn't as close to dying by a fall, she wasn't out of the woods yet. Or tunnel, in this case.

"I'll make sure you get to the helicopter," Cole said.

"You go first," Cyrus ordered. "That way, if they get trigger happy, they'll shoot you and not your precious doctor."

Cole led the way to the light at the end of the tunnel.

Ezekiel, Dalton and Rebecca had moved out ahead of them. The cages were empty. It was just the three of them as Cole emerged from the tunnel into the bright light of day.

Cole turned to Cyrus. "I need to talk to the man with the radio to have the helicopter land to pick you up."

The tip of Cyrus's knife had pricked the skin on Staci's neck. A single drop of blood dripped downward.

Cole swallowed a sudden surge of anger. Now wasn't the time to blow a gasket. Cyrus only had to dig a little deeper and he could sever her carotid artery. Then no amount of medical support could save her.

Cyrus tipped his chin. "Make it fast. My hand is getting tired of holding this knife."

"Father," Rebecca called out. "Let Dr. Miller go. Please."

"You. Are. Dead. To. Me," Cyrus bit out. He didn't turn toward his daughter or look at the tears in her eyes.

Cole couldn't imagine throwing away the love of a child. He'd give anything to have Tyler back. He hurried toward Jake.

His new boss met him halfway. "I take it he wants to negotiate?"

Cole nodded. "He wants to be flown out of here before the authorities arrive."

"Where to?" Jake asked, pulling his handheld radio off the clip on his vest.

"He'll let the pilot know as soon as they're in the air."

Jake's lips pressed into a line. "It's up to Jim Bob. It's his chopper and his life."

Cole met Jake's gaze. "It was that or he was going to throw her to her death down a mine shaft."

Jake nodded. "Roger." He turned away and spoke into the handheld radio. After what felt like an eternity, he turned back and gave Cole a brief nod.

The hovering helicopter lowered until it touched down on a plateau just above the mine entrance a hundred yards from where Cyrus stood with his knife poking a hole in Staci's neck.

Cole returned to the former leader of the Glory Valley community. "Ready?"

He nodded, his gaze darting to the other members of the Brotherhood Protectors. "Who are you?" he asked.

"It doesn't matter," Cole said. "All you need to worry about is getting on that helicopter."

Cyrus's eyes narrowed. "What's the catch?"

Cole held up his hands. "No catch. Just get on the helicopter and let the pilot know where you want to go."

The valley man's lip curled. "Lead the way."

Cole exchanged a glance with Staci.

Her eyes were wide and frightened.

He wanted to take away the pain and fear and punch the shit out of Cyrus for making her feel that way. Staci was kind and caring. She gave so much of herself to others, expecting nothing in return. Having come to his valley to offer her expertise to the people who lived here, she didn't deserve what Cyrus was doing to her.

One hundred yards.

As Cole walked the one hundred yards to where the helicopter waited, blades spinning, he went over and over the options for freeing Staci and keeping Cyrus from climbing aboard the aircraft. Every option had the huge risk of Cyrus's knife digging deeper.

They reached the helicopter, and Cole still hadn't figured out what he could do to keep Cyrus from taking off with Staci and the helicopter.

Cole turned to Cyrus and winged it. "You have your helicopter. You don't need Dr. Miller anymore."

Cyrus snorted. "I thought you were a lot smarter than that. Of course, I need the doctor. She's my ticket out of the country. Without her, I wouldn't have left the tunnel."

"I'll make a deal with you," Cole said. "Take me instead of the doctor."

"Again," Cyrus shook his head. "I thought you were smarter than that. The doctor is a lot less trouble, I'm sure, than you. She comes with me until I'm safely out of the country. Now, step aside. My hand is getting shaky. I'd hate for it to slip."

"It's okay," Staci said. "I'll be all right."

She wouldn't be all right. Cyrus was an insane psychopath. He'd kill her when she no longer served a purpose.

"Get on the helicopter," Cyrus ordered and pushed her forward, his hand on her shoulder, the knife pressed to her neck.

Cole couldn't get into a position where he could knock the knife out of the man's hand without him stabbing the blade into Staci's neck. He'd talked the man off the ledge of the shaft and convinced him to bring Staci out of the tunnel. Now, he could only step away and pray for a miracle.

Cole caught movement in the corner of his eye. He spun, but not soon enough to do anything.

Rebecca raced forward. "Daddy, don't go!"

When Cyrus glanced over his shoulder at the sound of his daughter's voice, Rebecca raised the taser gun she carried and shot the prongs into her father's back.

Immediately, Cyrus's muscles gave way, the knife fell from his fingers, and he dropped to the ground. The man's eyes rolled back in his head, and he lay still.

Cole rushed forward, stepped over the inert man and wrapped his arms around Staci.

She clung to him, her heart pounding hard enough that Cole could feel it against his chest. "I did not want to get on that helicopter," she said.

"I couldn't think of any way to keep him from taking you. Not when he had that knife to your throat." He stepped back and looked at the mark on her neck. "I wanted to kill the bastard," he said through clenched teeth. He brushed his lips across hers and sighed. "I died a thousand deaths in that tunnel. First, because I couldn't find you. And then, as you were standing at the edge of that shaft."

"I'm not going to lie. I had moments of pure terror." She laughed shakily and looked down at the man who'd caused so much grief. As she stared down at Cyrus, her brow dipped.

Staci dropped to a squat and touched two fingers to the base of Cyrus's throat.

Rebecca stood beside her father, the taser gun hanging limply from her fingertips. "I couldn't let him take you," she said hoarsely.

Staci didn't respond. She didn't feel a pulse. She leaned her head against his chest and listened for a heartbeat.

Nothing.

"His heart stopped." Staci rolled him over flat on his back and performed CPR. For the next thirty minutes, she worked on Cyrus, non-stop.

The sheriff arrived followed by an ambulance. The emergency medical technicians moved Cyrus to a stretcher, still working on him. They would continue until a medical evacuation helicopter could fly in to airlift him to a hospital.

Cole slipped an arm around Staci and pulled her against him. "You're an amazing human."

"Why?" she asked.

"The man tried to kill you." Cole shook his head. "I wanted to kill him. Yet you tried to save his life."

"I'm a doctor. I treat the sick or injured no matter who they are or what they've done. I took an oath."

"Oath or no oath, you'd do it anyway. It's who you are. I love that about you." He turned her in his arms and brushed his lips across her forehead. "Are you ready to get out of here?"

"After we're sure everyone is taken care of," she said.

Mark had been loaded onto a stretcher. He would be transported by road to the nearest hospital. They'd offered to airlift him with Cyrus. Mark didn't want to be anywhere near the man who'd stolen weeks of his life and terrorized his son.

Dalton stood by Rebecca as they loaded his father into the back of the ambulance.

The EMT held the door. "Are you coming with your father?"

Dalton nodded. "Yes, sir." He faced Rebecca, cupped her cheek and said, "I won't forget you."

She nodded and echoed, "I won't forget you." She gave him a weak, watery smile. "See you at college in a few years?"

He grinned. "You bet. And you have my address in Colorado Springs. If you get a chance, come visit. I'd love to show you my hometown."

"I'd like that very much." She leaned up on her

toes and kissed his cheek. "Thank you for being my friend."

"Thank you for saving my life."

She shrugged. "I couldn't let the boy who gave me my first kiss die. What kind of hero would I be?"

"You're the best." He bent and kissed her lips, and then turned and jumped into the back of the ambulance with his father.

The EMT closed the door, and they drove away.

Cole's heart ached for Rebecca.

"Young love is always so poignant," Staci whispered, leaning into Cole. "I hope they used the protection we found in the shack."

"You think they went that far?"

"Maybe." Staci turned into his arms with a teasing smile. "The shack was a pretty amazing place."

"Mmm. Agreed. However, I bet we can find a place with a softer mattress and gas heat."

She sighed. "It won't be the same." She looked up into his eyes. "There's something about that sex-against-the-wall kind of thing that gets the blood pumping."

He hugged her close. "I'm sure we can find ways to keep it interesting."

"I'm intrigued," she said, walking her fingers up the front of his shirt.

Jake approached them. "The county sheriff and the state police will wrap this up. You two ready to catch a ride home?"

"Almost," Staci said. "I have one more person to talk to before we leave." She glanced up at Cole. "I'll be right back."

"I'm not sure I feel comfortable letting you out of my sight," Cole said. "I almost lost you."

"I won't be out of your sight." Staci tipped her head toward a sheriff's deputy talking with Rebecca's mother. "I see Elizabeth. I want to make sure Rebecca is going to be okay."

Cole's chest tightened. "Be careful. I'm not sure I trust her."

"I will. I'm not sure I trust her, either." She hurried over to the deputy as the man slipped handcuffs on Elizabeth's wrists.

Staci wasn't surprised. Elizabeth had known what was happening. Staci suspected she was the one who'd cooked the meals for the prisoners. The woman couldn't deny her knowledge and complicity.

"Elizabeth," she said as she approached the older woman.

The older woman drew in a deep breath and let it out slowly, her lips tight, a sadness in her eyes. "I'm sorry about what happened," she said. "I want you to know I did not agree with everything my husband said or did. I am guilty of taking the path of least resistance when I should've stood up to him."

"Are they arresting you as an accessory?" Staci asked.

Elizabeth nodded.

"Get a good lawyer," Staci said. "Though you did wrong and didn't stop it from happening, this community needs you and your skills as a midwife."

She shrugged. "I doubt they'll ever get another doctor to come. Especially if they get wind of what we did to you. It was wrong. You did so much for us, and we repaid you by holding you hostage and threatening to kill you. I'm sorry."

"Apology accepted." Staci glanced toward Rebecca talking to one of the deputies. "What's going to happen to Rebecca while you and Cyrus are away?"

"She's going to stay with Naomi to help her with the baby."

Staci smiled. "She's good with babies and children, just not ready for her own. If she needs a place to stay, I'd welcome her into my home any day."

Elizabeth's eyes glazed with tears. "Thank you. Don't be surprised if I send her your way. I suspect that if I don't, she'll leave anyway."

Staci nodded. Elizabeth might know her daughter better than they'd given her credit for. "The offer is open," Staci said. "She's a good girl who deserves happiness."

Elizabeth's gaze fixed on her daughter. "I had three miscarriages before I had Rebecca. I want only the best for my child. I didn't know I was pushing her away. I should've tried harder."

The deputy opened the back door of his service vehicle, and Elizabeth climbed in.

When Staci turned, Cole was behind her. He opened his arms, and she stepped into his embrace.

"You know," she said, "through all of this, it was your voice in the darkness that made me stronger. You made me believe there was a way out."

He held her tighter and loosened his hold to tip up her head. His gaze held hers. "Your voice in the darkness helped me to see the light again. It was there all along, I just had to step into it. Thank you for reminding me I have a life to live."

"Your wife, your child, your friend—they all would've wanted you to be happy."

"I know that. Hell, I knew that." He gave her a crooked smile that melted her all the way to her core. "I didn't think I deserved that happiness when their lives ended so soon and mine didn't."

"You're a good man, Cole." Staci reached up to cup his cheek. "You deserve all the happiness life has to give.

He turned his face into her palm. "I don't know about that. All I know is that you make me feel things I didn't think I'd ever feel again."

"Before my mother died, she made me promise not to grieve too long. She wanted me to live the life given to me. You never know when your time is up. She wanted me to live like every day might be my last. No regrets." Staci swallowed hard on the lump rising in her throat. "My mother told me she had no regrets. She wanted that for me."

"Your mother was a wise woman. I wish I had met her."

Her eyes filled, clouding her vision. "You would've loved her. Everyone did." Staci blinked back the tears and lifted her chin. "I'm ready."

He grinned. "For what?"

Staci flung her arms wide. "For whatever life has to offer." She couldn't believe that after all the horror, fear and stress of the last few days, she could feel so happy. Most of that had to do with the man who'd come to her rescue.

He smiled and took her hand. "Come. There are some people I want you to meet."

Cole led her toward the waiting helicopter. The engine had been shut down after the sheriff and state police arrived. The five men who'd dropped down from the helicopter to join the fight against the valley men stood with a grizzled man wearing a headset halfcocked off one ear.

Cole led her to a tall, broad-shouldered man with black hair and brown eyes. The man stepped forward with a decided limp and held out his hand. "You must be Dr. Staci Miller."

She nodded and grasped his hand with a smile. "I am."

Cole leaned close to her. "Staci, this is Jake Cogburn, head of the Brotherhood Protectors Colorado division...my boss."

Jake tipped his head as he gave her hand a firm

shake. "It's a pleasure to meet you, Dr. Miller. I've heard good things about your work with the medically underserved in our state."

"And this is Max Thornton, one of the members of my team." Cole lifted his chin toward a sandy-blond-haired man with gray eyes, who was almost as tall as Jake and equally broad around the shoulders.

The man held out his hand. "My friends call me Thorn." She laid her hand in his, and he gave it a firm shake. "My woman says I'm a thorn in her side, but I know she loves me. Nice to meet the doc. Glad we got here in time for the party."

"I'm glad you did, too," Staci said with a smile.

Jake turned to the other men. "Cole is so new to the team, with Dr. Miller being his first assignment, he hasn't met the other members." He waved toward another tall man with black hair and blue eyes. "Dr. Miller, Cole, meet Cage Weaver, former Army Ranger, now a member of the Brotherhood Protectors."

Cage shook hands with Staci and Cole. "Glad to meet you both. And, Cole, welcome to the team. I think you'll like it with us."

"Thank you," Cole said. "I already do."

"And this is Sawyer Johnson, former Navy SEAL. This man has wicked sniper skills."

"Welcome aboard," Sawyer said as he shook Cole's hand. When he took Staci's, he nodded politely. "Glad to meet you, Dr. Miller."

"Lorenzo Ramos, meet Cole and Dr. Miller," Jake said. "Enzo was with the 10th Special Forces Group before he joined us."

Enzo shook hands with them both.

Everyone turned to the pilot.

"Our angel of mercy for the day is a friend of the team's landlord, Gunny Tate, and former Marine Force Recon, our pilot, Jim Bob McNamara."

The older guy held out his hand to Staci. "Most folks call me JB Mac. Pleased to meet you, ma'am."

Staci smiled at the man with the shock of silver-gray hair standing on end and a days-old white scruff of a beard. "Did you fly helicopters for the Marines?" she asked.

"Oh, hell no. They wouldn't let us play with the big toys."

Jake grinned, "From what Gunny told us, JB Mac learned how to fly after leaving the Marines."

JB Mac puffed out his chest. "That's right. You *can* teach old dogs new tricks. I'm proof of that." He waved a hand toward the helicopter that looked like one that had been a military aircraft at one time. Painted that particular shade of dull green, it appeared to have seen many better days. "Didn't get my helicopter flying license until I was forty-four. Didn't get the old rust bucket until I was fifty, as a gift to myself for living a half a century. She don't look like much, but I rescued her from being dumped in a boneyard and nursed her back to the beauty she is now."

Jake laughed. "Believe me, looks aren't everything. That bird can fly."

"Thank goodness," Cole said. "Otherwise, I'd still be the lone man fighting off every able-bodied man in Glory Valley." Cole reached for JB Mac's hand and pulled him into a hug. "Thank you for bringing my backup."

The pilot pounded Cole's back. "Glad to be of assistance. Besides, I needed the hours to keep my license current."

Jake clapped his hands together. "If everyone is ready, JB Mac has promised us the scenic tour back to Colorado Springs."

"Damn right." JB Mac grinned. "In Colorado, there ain't nothing but scenic tours. All aboard for the train back to the Springs!" He climbed into the pilot's seat.

Cole handed Staci up into the aircraft and settled her on a bench seat. After helping her with the safety straps and headset, he sat beside her, buckled in, and settled his own headset over his ears. Then he smiled and took her hand.

Jake claimed the co-pilot seat. The rest of the guys coiled their ropes, stowed them and claimed places on the bench seats, strapping in.

The engine roared to life.

As the rotors spun, Staci held onto Cole's hand. "This is my first time going up in a helicopter."

"This is my first time holding a woman's hand while in a helicopter." He grinned. "Life is full of firsts and adventure."

Staci squeezed his hand as the aircraft lifted off the ground. The chopper circled the valley one last time.

Staci stared down at what appeared to be a serene valley with quaint homes, cows and farmland. The mine building stood out against the mountainside. The valley, like the mine, had darkness running in veins throughout it. It also had strains of gold if you bothered to dig through the hard rock to get to it.

She glanced over at Cole and smiled.

He squeezed her hand. "Why the smile?"

"I was thinking that in the thick, impenetrable rock of that mountain, I found unimaginable riches."

Enzo leaned forward. "You found gold?"

Heat filled Staci's cheeks. She'd forgotten they could all hear what she was saying. "I found better. I found a…friend."

Cole lifted her hand and pressed his lips to her fingertips. "I'm hoping you found more than just a friend."

"Dude," Enzo shook his head. "If there's one thing I've learned…you don't rush the woman. When she's ready for more, she'll let you know."

"True," Sawyer agreed. "You've known each other

how long? A couple of days? It's too soon. Give it time."

"I disagree," Cage said. "It doesn't matter how long you know her...a month, a week, a day...when you know she's the one, she's the one, no matter how long you wait to satisfy a timeline."

"Right?" Jake turned to look over his shoulder. "I knew RJ was the one for me within a couple of days."

"With Carmen, it was love at first sight," JB Mac's gruff voice said into Staci's ears. "With Donna, I knew within a day. Lola has taken me a month."

Jake frowned at JB Mac. "We're trying to make a case for true, long-lasting love."

JB Mac gave Jake a puzzled look. "What? That's what I was doing. My first wife and I would've been married nearly forty years if she hadn't died in childbirth. She left me a son who reminds me of her every day. He flies F22s for the Air Force. Met my second wife at my son's high school graduation. Knew she was for me after two dates. Loved her until she passed with stage 4 breast cancer. Still love her and my first wife. Took me longer to let myself love Lola. It hurts to lose the ones you love. But she was patient, and I finally went with my heart. Been married now for three years. We're still on our honeymoon." He grinned back at Staci. "If you know, don't waste time you can be together. You never know how long you have."

Staci's cheeks heated. "I'm not saying until he says," she murmured.

Apparently, her words were loud enough for the others to hear.

"Well, Cole?" Sawyer cocked an eyebrow. "You gonna keep the doc waiting?"

"Yeah, you gonna make her sweat for a day, a week, a month?" Cage asked.

Thorn laughed. "No pressure, man. Just a team of guys and one pretty lady hanging on the answer."

"I'm not hanging," Staci assured him. "I know we just met and need time to get to know things about each other like what's our favorite meal, are you a dog person or a cat person, what our favorite colors are and what sports teams we follow."

He gripped her hands in his. "Steak, dogs, blue and the Broncos. I know I like you, and if I'm not already in love with you, I don't know what this heart-pounding, breath-catching feeling is."

"Altitude," Enzo said

Cage elbowed him in the side. "Shh. Let him continue."

"I don't care if you're vegan, love cats and the color purple, or if you back the Dallas Cowboys. I can live with all of that. What I can't live without is you and your voice in the dark." He stared into her eyes. "I say we see where this goes."

She nodded. "Agreed. I'm not sure about love at

first sight, but I can attest to love at first word in the dark."

Cole peeled his headset off and removed hers. Then he cupped her cheeks and crushed her lips in a kiss that melted her all the way to her toes.

Over the roar of the engine, she could hear the cheers and clapping of the Brotherhood Protectors team.

She'd found the one.

EPILOGUE

Two weeks later

COLE LAID a single red rose at the base of Lisa's headstone and a white one in front of the smaller headstone beside it. "I'll never stop loving either of you, and I'll never forget what we had. You are forever in my heart. What happened in Glory Valley and since hasn't diminished what I feel for you two. If anything, it has made my love stronger and made me realize I still have room in my heart to love again."

He held out his hand.

Staci stepped closer and laid her palm in his.

"You were lucky to have loved so deeply," she said. "It makes me appreciate you even more and honored that you've found that room in your heart for me." She leaned against him, holding tightly to his hand.

"She would've wanted me to love again, to have a family and be happy."

"She sounds like she was an amazing person," Staci said. "But then she would have to be for you to love her."

"I miss them," he said. "I always will."

"Are you sure you're ready to start over?" Staci asked.

He turned to pull her into his arms. "Absolutely positive." He kissed her soundly and leaned back, a frown pulling at his forehead. "Are you?"

Her grin stretched across her face, and her eyes shone in the sunlight. "Never more certain of anything in my life." Then her smile faded. "Are you ready to go for the whole enchilada?" She laughed shakily. "Look at me trying to sound hip." She looked away, her gaze going to the tiny headstone. "Are you ready for a family? Because I want children. At least two, maybe more." Her gaze met his, her brow creased. "If you don't want children, that might be a deal-breaker. And I don't want to lose you now that I've found you."

He touched a finger to her lips and gave her a gentle smile. "I love how you talk a lot when you're nervous. Sweetheart, you have nothing to be nervous about. I want children. The more the merrier. More than that, I want children with you. I know you'll be a wonderful mother, and you have skills to see them through colds, scrapes and other childhood ailments. I love you, Dr. Staci Miller." He fished in his pocket, glanced down at Lisa's headstone and shrugged. "I wasn't going to do this here, but I think Lisa would approve. She would have loved you.

"I had planned to take you up to Pike's Peak to do this, but as a wise old man once said, when you know, you don't want to waste any more time that you can be together." He dropped to one knee, took her hand and stared up at her.

Staci's eyes filled with tears.

"Staci, you saved me from darkness and showed me the light of love. Will you be my wife?"

Tears streamed down her face as she dropped to her knees in front of him. "Yes. I will."

When he removed the ring from the box and reached for her hand, she closed her fingers around his. "Before we seal the deal with a kiss, I need to tell you something...I don't think it will make a difference, but you should know."

He laughed. "Nothing could change my mind."

"Hold that thought," she said. "Remember the condoms we found in the shack?"

His brow wrinkled. "Yes."

"I know for a fact Rebecca and Dalton didn't use them or make love for that matter."

Cole shook his head. "I'm confused. What are you trying to say?"

"The condoms were faulty. Maybe extreme cold made them less effective. I don't know. All I do know is they didn't work."

"What does that have to do with Rebecca and Dalton?" he asked.

Staci laughed. "Nothing. It has everything to do with us."

Cole gripped her hands. "I'm trying, but I'm still clueless. What are you trying to say?"

"The condom we used was faulty. It didn't work." She met and held his gaze. "Cole, I'm pregnant."

He froze, his heart stopped and he didn't breathe for a full five seconds. Then her words hit like a tsunami. He bent over with the force of the emotions tumbling over and through him.

"Cole?" Staci touched his shoulder. "Breathe, Cole."

He drew in a deep breath and let it out.

Staci's hand dropped to her side. "I'm sorry. I should've told you this morning after I took the test and found out for myself. But I knew we were coming to visit Lisa and Tyler. I didn't want what was happening to me take away from this. I'm sorry."

Cole rose to his feet and pulled Staci up to stand with him. "Don't be sorry. I couldn't be happier."

Staci shook her head. "But you didn't seem to be happy."

"I am, and I love you even more." His face split in a grin so wide it almost hurt. "We're going to have a baby," he whispered. He took her hand in his and slipped a ring with a shiny diamond solitaire onto her finger.

"I wasn't sure you were ready," she said. "I mean we love each other, but a baby…"

"Will make our lives even more perfect. When can we get married?"

She laughed. "Whenever you like."

"I like now."

"We have to get a marriage license."

"Today," he said. "We'll get it today."

"We can't do it today. We're picking up my father in Denver and driving out to Glory Valley to get Rebecca. She's coming to live with me." She frowned. "How is that going to work? I can't tell her no just because we're getting married. Since they weren't able to save her father after his massive heart attack, and her mother will be in jail for at least a year, she needs someone who cares to look out for her wellbeing. I can't go back on my promise."

"I wouldn't want you to. We'll find a place big enough for a baby's room and a room for a teen. And yes, we're going to get Rebecca today." He drew in a breath and let it out. "Tomorrow, we'll get that marriage license. Can you find a dress by Saturday?"

She laughed. "I don't know. Maybe. Hell, I don't care if I do. I'll find something. I'm getting married. I'll go in my jeans if that's all I can find."

"You'd be beautiful in anything." He smiled. His

heart was so full he was afraid it might burst. He'd found love for the second time in his life. She was pregnant with their child.

With Staci by his side, he was ready to start living the rest of his life.

SOLDIER'S DUTY

IRON HORSE LEGACY BOOK #1

New York Times & USA Today
Bestselling Author

ELLE JAMES

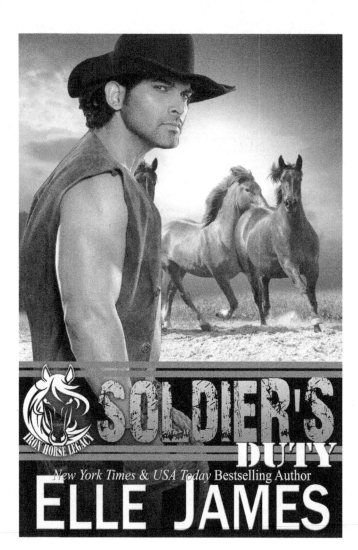

SOLDIER'S
DUTY

IRON HORSE LEGACY

New York Times & *USA Today* Bestselling Author

ELLE JAMES

CHAPTER 1

"As you all know, William Reed escaped from a prison transport yesterday." Sheriff Barron stood in front of a group of men and women who'd gathered around him at the side of the highway in the foothills of the Crazy Mountains on a blustery cold day in early April.

He continued, "We have security camera footage showing him stealing a car from a convenience store in Bozeman. The license plate of the vehicle he stole matches the license plate of the vehicle behind me." Sheriff Barron turned to the side and waved toward a vehicle half-hidden in the brush behind him. "The state police are on their way, and they're also sending a helicopter from Bozeman. But they aren't as familiar with the mountainous terrain as you are, and the weather might keep them from using the chopper. That's why I've asked you to bring your horses and ATVs. All of you know these mountains better than anyone. And you are the select group of people I trust most to handle this situation."

James McKinnon tugged up the collar of his coat around his chin to keep a blast of wintery wind from snaking down his neck. He listened silently as the sheriff explained why they were there. With each breath James took, he blew out a little cloud of steam.

Rucker, his bay gelding, pawed at the ground impatiently.

James had chosen Rucker because he was the most sure-footed of the horses in his stable. For the manhunt they were about to conduct, the gelding was the best bet. The Crazy Mountains could be as dangerous as the man they were searching for. And the weather wasn't helping.

The sheriff gave them a steely glance. "We don't know at this point whether or not Reed is armed but assume that he is."

James's hand went to the pistol in the holster he had strapped to his hip.

"Sheriff, what do you want us to do?" one of the men in the crowd called out.

The sheriff straightened, with his shoulders pushed back and his mouth set in a firm line. He stared at each of the people gathered around, making eye contact with each person. "Bring him in."

"And how do you want us to do that," another man called out.

The sheriff's chin lifted. "Most of you follow the news. Reed was in prison for multiple counts of murder. He killed two guards during the armored truck robbery. When he was cornered, he killed two cops. The man was serving a life sentence without parole.

"While being transported to a high-security prison, his transport vehicle ran off the road. The driver was killed on impact, but the guard in back with Reed wasn't. He was injured. Reed finished him off. Now, I'm not telling you to kill Reed, but if at any time you believe your life is in danger, shoot to kill the bastard. If at all possible, don't engage...report. Our primary goal is to bring Reed in before he hurts anyone else."

James's hands tightened into fists. He hadn't killed a man since he'd been a member of Delta Force more than two decades ago. Not that he'd become squeamish about killing a man in his old age, but it was just that he'd thought his people-killing days were over when he'd left the military.

The only killing he'd done lately was the occasional coyote in the chicken coop and deer or elk while hunting in the fall.

From the news reports he'd been following, he knew Reed had turned into a really bad character.

James was glad the bastard had headed into the mountains instead of the city. He reckoned that if the convict was cornered, he would take whatever hostage he could to get out of a situation.

James had left instructions with his wife and daughter to stay inside the ranch house and keep the doors locked. But he knew they were stubborn women and wouldn't stand by and leave the animals to fend for themselves, especially in bad weather. They'd venture out into the barnyard to feed the chickens, pigs, horses and goats to keep them from going hungry. With the winter weather making a reappearance, they'd likely put some of the livestock in the barn.

Which would leave them at risk of being captured if Reed circled back to the Iron Horse Ranch. Hopefully, they'd be smart and enlist the help of their ranch foreman, Parker Bailey.

Sheriff Barron held up a paper with an image of William Reed. James didn't need to see the picture. He knew Reed. However, others amongst them were newer to Eagle Rock and the county. "This is our man. Right now, we think he's up in the mountains. The longer he's free, the hungrier he'll get. It's imperative we bring him in quickly. All of our families' lives are in danger as long as he runs free."

"Then let's stop talking and start tracking," Marty Langley called out.

The sheriff nodded. "All right, then, gather

around the map. We're going to split up into different quadrants so we're not shooting at each other." Sheriff Barron spread a map over the hood of his SUV, and the group gathered around him. He gave instructions as to where each person would be during the hunt and what signal they should give if they found something. He handed out as many two-way radios as he had, distributing them to every other quadrant.

Once James had his assigned area, he mounted Rucker and rode into the mountains, his knee nudging the rifle in his scabbard, his hand patting the pistol on his hip.

He'd known Reed for years. When you lived in a small community, everyone knew everyone else. Some were better at keeping secrets than others but, for the most part, everyone knew everyone else's business.

Reed had been a regular guy, working in construction and hitting the bar at night. He'd been a ladies' man with a lot going for him. How had a guy like that ended up robbing an armored truck and killing the people driving it? What had driven Reed down the wrong path?

James could have been home with his wife of thirty-five wonderful years, holding her close in front of the fireplace, instead of riding out on a cold winter's night in search of a killer.

He knew he had it good. After twenty years in the

military, he'd settled in Montana on the land his father had passed down to him. He'd wanted his kids to have what he'd had growing up. Ranching had made him the man he was—unafraid of hard work, determined to make a difference, able to take on any challenge, no matter how physically or mentally difficult.

He'd been damned proud of his sons and daughter and how they'd taken to ranching like they'd been born to it. Even Angus, who'd been twelve when they'd moved to the Crazy Mountains of Montana. He'd been the first to learn to ride and show the other boys how wonderful it could be to have the wind in their faces, galloping across the pastures.

A cold wind whipped into James's face, bringing him back to the present and the bitterness of an early spring cold snap. Just when they'd thought spring had come and the snow had started to melt at the lower elevations, the jet stream had taken a violent shift downward, dipping south from Canada into the Rocky Mountains of Montana, dumping a foot of fresh snow all the way down into the valleys.

He nudged Rucker in the flanks, sending him up the path leading to a small canyon that crossed over a couple of ranches—including his, the Iron Horse Ranch.

He knew the area better than anyone, having lived

on the ranch as a child and as an adult since he'd returned from serving in the Army. As his father's only child, he'd inherited the ranch upon his father's death. Now, it was up to him to make it sustainable and safe for his family and ranch hands.

Again, he thought about his wife, Hannah, and his daughter, Molly, and worried for their safety.

Clouds sank low over the mountaintops, bringing with it more snow, falling in giant flakes. The wind drove them sideways, making it difficult to see the trail ahead.

About the time James decided to turn back, he'd entered the canyon. Sheer walls of rock blocked some of the wind and snow, making it a little easier to see the path in front of Rucker.

James decided to give the hunt a little more time before he gave up and returned to the highway where he'd parked his horse trailer.

He knew of several caves in the canyon suitable for a fugitive to hole up in during a brutal winter storm. They weren't much further along the trail, but they were higher up the slope. Snowcapped ridges rose up beside him. He was careful not to make any loud noises that might trigger an avalanche. Spending the next couple days in a cave wasn't something he wanted to do.

If he survived an avalanche, he could make do with the natural shelter until a rescue chopper could get into the canyon and fish him out. But Hannah and Molly would be sick with worry. James tried not to put himself in situations that made his sweet wife worry. Unfortunately, the Reed escape had worry written all over it. The man had escaped. He'd already proven he'd kill rather than go back to jail. He wouldn't go peacefully.

Rucker climbed higher up the side of the canyon wall, following a narrow path dusted in snow. The wind blew the majority of the flakes away, keeping the rocky ground fairly recognizable.

The trail had been there for as long as James could remember. His father had told him it was a trail created by the Native Americans who'd once used the caves for shelter over a century ago.

Rucker stumbled on a rock and lurched to the side.

James's heart skipped several beats as he held onto the saddle horn.

Once Rucker regained his balance, he continued up the slope, plodding along, the snow pelting his eyes. He shook his head and whinnied softly.

James patted the horse's neck. "It's okay. Only a little farther, and we'll head back to the barn." The weather in early April was unpredictable. It could stop snowing altogether or become a white-out blizzard in a matter of minutes.

The first in the row of caves James remembered

appeared ahead and up the slope to his left. He dropped down from his horse's back and studied the dark opening. If he recalled correctly, the cave was little more than five or six feet back into the mountain side. Not enough to protect a man from the cold wind and driving snow.

James grabbed Rucker's reins and moved on to the next cave, glancing up the side of the hill as he approached.

The hackles on the back of his neck rose to attention. Had he seen movement in the shadowy entrance?

He stopped beside a small tree growing out of the side of the hill and looped Rucker's reins loosely over a branch. The horse wouldn't attempt to pull free. Rucker knew to hold fast. A loud noise might scare him into bolting for the barn. Otherwise, he'd stay put until James returned.

Pulling his handgun from the holster, James started up the incline toward the cave, his focus on the entrance and the overhang of snow on the slope above the cave. With the recent melting and the added layer of fresh snow, the snow above the cave could easily become unstable. Anything, including a gust of wind, could trigger an avalanche, sending snow and rocks crashing down the hillside.

James hoped he'd left Rucker well out of the path of the potential avalanche. If the snow started down

ELLE JAMES

the side of the hill, James would be forced to run for the cave and take shelter there. Possibly with a killer.

More reason to get up to the cave, check it out and get back down to Rucker as soon as possible. He should have turned back when the snow got so thick he could barely see the trail. If one of his sons or daughter had continued on, he would have reamed them for their irresponsible behavior. And here he was doing what he would expect them to avoid.

However, since he was there, he would check the cave. Then he'd head straight back to the highway and home. The search for the fugitive could continue the next day, after the snowstorm ended. Reed wouldn't make much headway in the current weather, anyway.

With his plan in mind, James trudged up the hill to the cave. He had camped in this particular grotto one fall when he'd been caught in a storm while out hunting elk. It went back far enough into the mountain to protect him from the wind and rain and was open enough to allow him to build a fire. He'd even staged additional firewood in case he ever got caught in a storm again. Then at least, he'd have dry wood to build a warming fire.

If Reed was up in this canyon, this cave would be the perfect shelter from the current storm. The next one in line was harder to find and had a narrower entrance.

As he neared the mouth of the cavern, he drew on

his Delta Force training, treading lightly and keeping as much of his body out of direct line of fire as possible as he edged around the corner and peered into the shadows.

The sound of voices echoed softly from the darkness near the back of the cave. He smelled wood smoke before he spotted the yellow glow of a fire, shedding light on two figures standing nearby.

"Where is it?" one voice was saying, the tone urgent, strained.

"I'm not telling you. If I tell you, you have no reason to keep me alive."

James stiffened. He remembered having a conversation with Reed outside the hardware store in Eagle Rock several years ago. That husky, deep voice wasn't something a person forgot.

His pulse quickening, James knew he had to get back down the mountain to the sheriff and let him know what he'd found. They weren't supposed to engage, just report.

But he hadn't expected to find Reed with someone else. If he left and reported to the sheriff without identifying the other man and the two men managed to get out of the canyon before they were captured by the authorities, no one would know who was helping Reed.

"I got you out of there, the least you can do is share your secret."

"I put it somewhere no one will find it. If I die, it

goes to the grave with me," Reed said. "I did that on purpose. I can't trust anyone. If you want to know where it is, you'll have to get me out of Montana alive."

"I told you I would. You have my word. But you can't leave Montana without it."

"No, but I can leave Montana without you. If I've learned one thing in prison," Reed's voice grew deeper, "the only person you can trust is yourself."

"Damn it, Reed, we don't have time to dick around. Sheriff Barron has a posse combing the mountains. The only thing keeping them from finding you is the storm moving in. Get the money, and let's get the hell out of here."

James strained to see into the darkness, but the man with Reed had his back to the cave entrance and appeared to be wearing a knit ski hat. The voice was familiar, but he couldn't put his finger on who it was. He leaned into the cave a little more, waiting for the man to shift into a position where the fire would light up his face.

"You know, there's a bounty on your head," the man told Reed, in a threatening tone. "Maybe I don't want your bag of money. It's probably marked anyway. I could turn you in and collect the reward. I'd have the money and be a hero for saving the world from a killer."

Reed lunged toward the other man, knocking him back, his face even deeper in the shadows, or was it covered in a ski mask? "You dare threaten me?" He lifted the man off his feet and shoved him against the wall. "Do you know the hell I've lived in for the past thirteen years? I've seen men like you who've had their tongues carved out with a spoon. I didn't get out of prison to put up with the likes of you."

The man being held against the wall gagged, his feet scraping against the hard rock surface behind him.

James couldn't let Reed kill the other man, even if the other man happened to be the one who'd helped him escape from prison. Taking a deep breath, he called out, "Drop him, Reed, or I'll shoot."

The convict froze with his hand still gripping the other man's throat. "Guess you're gonna have to shoot." Then he spun, dragging his captive with him, and using his body as a shield.

Since his back was still to James, James couldn't see who it was.

"Go ahead," Reed taunted. "Shoot. This piece of shit deserves to die."

The man he held fumbled in his jacket pocket, pulled out something long and shiny and then shoved it toward Reed.

Reed gasped, his eyes widening. "Bastard," he said, his voice more of a wheeze. His grip loosened on his captive.

The man slumped to his knees and bent over.

Reed stood for a long moment, his hand curling

around the knife protruding from his chest. He gripped the handle and pulled it out. He stared at it, and then at James, and collapsed on top of the man he'd almost killed.

James rushed forward, jammed his handgun into his holster and felt for a pulse in Reed's neck. He had one, but it was faint and fluttering erratically.

The man beneath him, grunted and pushed at the bulk of the dead man weighing him down. "Help me," he said.

James grabbed Reed's arm and pulled him off the other man, laying him flat on his back.

Reed stared up at James, his eyes narrowing. He whispered something.

James leaned close, barely able to hear.

"Where the...snake...threads...needle's eye," Reed coughed, and blood dribbled out of the side of his mouth.

James pressed his hand to the wound in Reed's chest. Having seen similar wounds in Iraq, he figured the knife had damaged a major organ, and Reed wasn't going to make it out of that cave alive.

Reed raised a hand and clutched his collar in a surprisingly strong grip. "They'll never find it." He chuckled, a gurgling sound that caused more blood to ooze from the corner of his mouth. Then his hand dropped to his side, and his body went limp.

James pressed two fingers to the base of Reed's

throat, feeling for a pulse. When he felt none, he started to straighten.

Something cold and hard pressed to his temple. "Move, and I'll shoot."

His heart hammering against his ribs, James reached for the gun at his side. A cold feeling washed over him that had nothing to do with the gale-force winds blasting down through the canyon outside the walls of the cave.

His holster was empty. He couldn't believe he'd helped the other man, only to have him take his gun and turn it on him.

"What did Reed say before he died?" the man behind him demanded.

James held up his hands, shaking his head. "I don't remember."

"You better start, or you can join him in his cold place in hell."

"Seriously, I couldn't hear what he said. It was all garbled."

"He said something about a needle. I know you heard him. Tell me." The angry guy behind him fired the gun, hitting James in the right arm.

Pain knifed through his arm, and it hung limp against his side.

"Tell me, or I'll shoot again."

Outside, a rumbling sound made James forget about being shot at again. "If you want to get out of this cave alive, we have to leave now."

"I'm the one with the gun. I say when we leave."

"Then you'll have to shoot me, because I'm not going to be trapped in this cave by an avalanche." James lurched to his feet and started for the entrance.

Rocks and snow started to fall from the slope above the cave's entrance.

"Avalanche," James called out.

The entire hillside to the south of the cave seemed to be slipping downward toward the floor of the canyon.

"Stop, or I'll shoot again!" the man in the ski mask yelled.

"That's what got the avalanche started in the first place. If you shoot again, even more will come crashing down on us." James kept moving toward the cave entrance, looking north at a narrow trail leading out of the other side of the cave from where he'd entered. "If you want to live, you better follow me, and for the love of God, don't shoot again." He'd figure another way out of this mess, if he didn't bleed out first. For now, James knew he had to get the hell out of there. If they stayed inside the cave, they'd be trapped. If they hurried out the north end, they might make it away from the avalanche.

Rocks and snow pelted his back as he hurried across the slippery slope, praying the bulk of the avalanche was well on its way to the south. But more snow and rocks rushed toward him and the man holding a gun on him. His head light from blood loss,

James ran, stumbling and skidding across loose gravel and tripping over small boulders. A rush of snow and debris scooped his feet out from under him and sent him sliding down the slope. He fought to keep his head above the snow. Then he crashed into something hard and everything went black.

ABOUT THE AUTHOR

ELLE JAMES also writing as MYLA JACKSON is a *New York Times* and *USA Today* Bestselling author of books including cowboys, intrigues and paranormal adventures that keep her readers on the edges of their seats. When she's not at her computer, she's traveling, snow skiing, boating, or riding her ATV, dreaming up new stories. Learn more about Elle James at www.ellejames.com

Website | Facebook | Twitter | GoodReads | Newsletter | BookBub | Amazon

Or visit her alter ego Myla Jackson at mylajackson.com
Website | Facebook | Twitter | Newsletter

Follow Me!
www.ellejames.com
ellejamesauthor@gmail.com

ALSO BY ELLE JAMES

Justice Burning (#2)

Smoldering Desire (#3)

Hellfire in High Heels (#4)

Playing With Fire (#5)

Up in Flames (#6)

Total Meltdown (#7)

Declan's Defenders

Marine Force Recon (#1)

Show of Force (#2)

Full Force (#3)

Driving Force (#4)

Tactical Force (#5)

Disruptive Force (#6)

Mission: Six

One Intrepid SEAL

Two Dauntless Hearts

Three Courageous Words

Four Relentless Days

Five Ways to Surrender

Six Minutes to Midnight

Hearts & Heroes Series

Wyatt's War (#1)

Mack's Witness (#2)

Ronin's Return (#3)

Sam's Surrender (#4)

Take No Prisoners Series

SEAL's Honor (#1)

SEAL'S Desire (#2)

SEAL's Embrace (#3)

SEAL's Obsession (#4)

SEAL's Proposal (#5)

SEAL's Seduction (#6)

SEAL'S Defiance (#7)

SEAL's Deception (#8)

SEAL's Deliverance (#9)

SEAL's Ultimate Challenge (#10)

Texas Billionaire Club

Tarzan & Janine (#1)

Something To Talk About (#2)

Who's Your Daddy (#3)

Love & War (#4)

Billionaire Online Dating Service

The Billionaire Husband Test (#1)

The Billionaire Cinderella Test (#2)

The Billionaire Bride Test (#3)

The Billionaire Daddy Test (#4)

The Billionaire Matchmaker Test (#5)

The Billionaire Glitch Date (#6)

The Billionaire Perfect Date (#7) coming soon

The Billionaire Replacement Date (#8) coming soon

The Billionaire Wedding Date (#9) coming soon

Ballistic Cowboy

Hot Combat (#1)

Hot Target (#2)

Hot Zone (#3)

Hot Velocity (#4)

Cajun Magic Mystery Series

Voodoo on the Bayou (#1)

Voodoo for Two (#2)

Deja Voodoo (#3)

Cajun Magic Mysteries Books 1-3

SEAL Of My Own

Navy SEAL Survival

Navy SEAL Captive

Navy SEAL To Die For

Navy SEAL Six Pack

Hot Demon Nights (#1)

Demon's Embrace (#2)

Tempting the Demon (#3)

Lords of the Underworld

Witch's Initiation (#1)

Witch's Seduction (#2)

The Witch's Desire (#3)

Possessing the Witch (#4)

Stealth Operations Specialists (SOS)

Nick of Time

Alaskan Fantasy

Boys Behaving Badly Anthology

Rogues (#1)

Blue Collar (#2)

Pirates (#3)

Stranded (#4)

First Responder (#5)

Shadow Assassin

Blown Away

Warrior's Conquest

Enslaved by the Viking Short Story

Conquests

Smokin' Hot Firemen

Protecting the Colton Bride

Protecting the Colton Bride & Colton's Cowboy Code

Heir to Murder

Secret Service Rescue

High Octane Heroes

Haunted

Engaged with the Boss

Cowboy Brigade

Time Raiders: The Whisper

Bundle of Trouble

Killer Body

Operation XOXO

An Unexpected Clue

Baby Bling

Under Suspicion, With Child

Texas-Size Secrets

Cowboy Sanctuary

Lakota Baby

Dakota Meltdown

Beneath the Texas Moon

Made in the USA
Monee, IL
14 April 2022

94753243R00138